OU
DARE?

For the real William (Bill) Prosser – thanks!

PENGUIN BOOKS

UK | USA | Canada | Ireland | Australia
India | New Zealand | South Africa | China

Penguin Books is part of the Penguin Random House group of companies
whose addresses can be found at global.penguinrandomhouse.com.

Penguin
Random House
Australia

1 3 5 7 9 10 8 6 4 2

Cover and internal design by Tony Palmer
© Penguin Group (Australia)
Illustrations by Guy Shield
Printed and bound in Australia by Griffin Press,
an accredited ISO AS/NZS 14001
Environmental Management Systems printer.

National Library of Australia Cataloguing-in-Publication
data is available.

ISBN 978 0 14 330802 7

MIX
Paper from
responsible sources
FSC   FSC® C009448
www.fsc.org

puffin.com.au

1915
DO YOU DARE?

JIMMY'S WAR
S. CLARK

PUFFIN BOOKS

AUSTRALIA
1915

WA

Perth

N

W   E

S

arwin

NT

QLD

Brisbane

SA

NSW

Sydney

Adelaide

FCT

Melbourne

Where this story takes place

TAS

Hobart

1

Jimmy glanced up at the setting sun and forced his feet down harder on the bicycle pedals. One more delivery and he could head back to Mr Brown's grocery store. Old Brown had promised him a quarter pound of minced beef if he did two extra deliveries, and it'd been a few days since he and Mum had eaten meat for tea.

Not that the mince would be fresh. Old Brown only gave him stuff that was on the edge of going off. Still, Mum was a marvel at turning even scraps into tasty dinners. Jimmy's stomach rumbled and he pedalled faster, swinging out as he reached the corner of Stephen Street and half-skidding around the corner.

A large black shape loomed suddenly in the twilight and threw its hands up with a scream. Jimmy wrenched at the handlebars of the big bicycle and swerved, slamming on his brakes. But it was too late. His back wheel skidded on the bluestone cobbles and he thumped into the dark shape. It fell back onto the footpath and he fell on top of it, his leg twisted under him.

The shape groaned and pushed at him with soft, pudgy hands. Jimmy scrambled up, his heart thudding under his ribs. What had he done? Who had he hit?

The black shape slowly sat up and focused on him. It was Mrs Langley, the widow who ran the haberdashery shop, and she had a tongue on her like a whip. Jimmy braced himself.

'Jimmy Miller!' she screeched. 'You're nothing but a larrikin! You could've killed me.'

'Yes, Mrs Langley, sorry, Mrs Langley.' Sweat dripped down Jimmy's neck as he tried to smile at the grumpy old woman. 'It's just . . .

I was in a hurry. I was on a delivery.'

'Delivery for what?'

'Mr Brown's shop. I was taking . . . '

Uh oh. He looked around. The potatoes were strewn everywhere and the bags of sugar and flour had split and were spilt across the road. He felt sick. Mr Brown would surely take the cost out of his wages, which were measly enough already.

'Is that right?' Mrs Langley refused his hand and got to her feet. She pointed at the potatoes and ripped paper bags. 'Well, you can pick that up and come with me, young man. I'll teach you to ride like a ruffian and run down a poor woman like me.'

Jimmy bent to collect the potatoes, one at a time, and then the paper bags. Surely she didn't mean it? Maybe he could tell her about Arthur being away at the war, and how Mum was pining, and how he desperately needed the wages from Mr Brown. But one look at Mrs Langley's angry face and he knew it would be wasted.

She made him carry her large black purse in his bicycle basket and walk behind her, all the way to Mr Brown's shop in Anderson Street. The black rose bobbed angrily in her hat as she scolded him.

'You should know better than to ride like that,' she said. 'Your brother, Arthur, never behaved like this. You should be taking a leaf out of his book.'

Yes, yes, Jimmy thought. Everyone in Yarraville loved Arthur. Half the girls had cried when he enlisted, and it seemed like their mums had, too. All the footy supporters sobbed in their beer at the thought of losing Arthur from the team. Clearly, even Mrs Langley thought Jimmy was a poor substitute.

Mr Brown kept his shop open late, trying to compete with the bigger grocery on the corner. He spotted Mrs Langley at the door and came rushing out to serve her.

'This larrikin,' Mrs Langley declared, pointing at Jimmy, 'was riding dangerously and ran right into me. I could've been badly hurt!'

Jimmy secretly thought someone as fat as Mrs Langley had far too much padding for that. He was the one who was hurt – his leg ached, and the back of his neck burned from the late autumn sun. He opened his mouth to say sorry yet again, but Mr Brown didn't give him the chance.

'I'm terribly sorry, Mrs Langley.' Mr Brown cringed, wringing his hands. 'It's so hard to get good help. These lads . . . '

Hang on, I work hard! Jimmy thought.

'I've a good mind to shop at Brigalows,' Mrs Langley said.

'Oh, no, no, no!' Mr Brown gasped. His face paled and he glared at Jimmy. 'No need for that, Mrs Langley. The boy shall be sacked at once.'

'At once?'

'Right away, Mrs Langley!' Mr Brown turned angrily to Jimmy and suddenly caught sight of the split bags in Jimmy's basket. 'And you owe me for that flour and sugar, boy, so don't go asking for your wages, either. Now, be off with you.'

Jimmy opened his mouth to argue that it had all been an accident, but two grown-ups glaring at him like he was a criminal was too much for him. He turned and walked away, wheeling his bicycle, shame and anger smashing around inside him. Mr Brown was just an old fart, and Mrs Langley was a nasty old crow!

When he reached the first glowing street lamp, he stopped to check his bicycle. Please, don't let it be damaged, he prayed. It had been his dad's, and then his brother Arthur's, and now it was his. It was Jimmy's only real link to Dad, and he kept it spick and span. He was growing into it, but it was still a heavy old thing to pedal around Yarraville.

Jimmy's route home was down Ballarat Street, past two pubs, both of which tended to have drunks spilling out their doors by tea-time. He wheeled his bicycle, head down, lost in misery. How was he going to tell Mum he'd lost his job? Even though Mr Brown paid a pittance, they relied on his few shillings and hand-outs.

At the second pub, a voice called to Jimmy from the back door. 'G'day, there.'

Jimmy paused uncertainly. It was Bill Prosser, the local bookie and crim, his beady eyes gleaming.

'Aren't you Arthur Miller's brother?' Bill beckoned Jimmy closer.

Jimmy hesitated. The stink of stale beer wafted out from the half-open pub door. 'You know Arthur?' he said.

'Sure do.' Prosser had a funny smile on his face.

'Good-o,' Jimmy said. 'Um, Mr Prosser, I gotta get –'

'Call me Bill,' the bookie said. 'Listen, I've got an errand needs running. Urgent, like.

I can pay you a shilling.'

Jimmy thought for a moment. A shilling was half as much as he earned from stingy Mr Brown in a week! But he had heard about Bill Prosser. 'Up to no good' and 'Bound for gaol, you mark my words' were some of the things he'd been told. Prosser took bets on the horse races, which was something the coppers got you for. Even worse, he was rumoured to have done a few robberies as well. If Bill wanted Jimmy to run some bets, the coppers would be after Jimmy in no time, even if he was just a kid.

'It's nothin' to do with the betting,' Bill said. 'I promise. It's something for me mum. She lives the other side of Somerville Road.'

Somerville Road was in the opposite direction to home. By the time he rode there and then home again, it'd be well after dark. Mum would be on the front verandah or pacing the street. Since Arthur had gone off to the war, she acted as though Jimmy had to be wrapped in cottonwool. It was as though she couldn't see how hard he worked, how he'd taken Arthur's place in a lot of ways. She only had eyes for the letterbox, waiting for a letter from Arthur.

This was a whole shilling . . . Mum would be upset about Mr Brown sacking him. But maybe this would kind of make up for it. For today, anyway.

'All right,' Jimmy said. 'What is it?'

'Just a parcel.'

'A parcel of what?'

'Part of that shilling means no questions,' Bill said sharply. 'But if you must know, it's meat for Mum's tea.'

'Oh. Hand it over then.'

Bill fetched the parcel from inside the pub; Jimmy shoved it into his basket, pocketed the shilling and set off again down Ballarat Street.

Bill shouted after him, 'You make sure you go straight there, Jimmy boy.'

'I will,' Jimmy yelled. He pedalled as hard as

he could, not caring if he ran into Mrs Langley again. What difference would it make now?

Dusk had fallen and fog drifted across the flats from the river. At Mrs Prosser's house, he banged on the door, short and sharp.

'Who's this kicking my door down?' Mrs Prosser loomed in the doorway, and from behind her the delicious smell of meat roasting wafted out. Jimmy's stomach groaned.

'Parcel for you from Bill,' Jimmy said. He pushed it into her hands, ready to rush off again.

'Hang on,' Mrs Prosser said. She fumbled in a small purse that was on the side table in the hallway, and handed Jimmy a sixpence.

'Gee, thanks,' Jimmy said. For a brief moment, he wondered if it really was meat in the parcel, since she had a roast in the oven. But he pushed the thought aside quickly. Too late to worry about that. Time to go. He had no light on his bicycle and he'd have to navigate his way towards home very carefully, especially down the end of his street where the big puddles were.

Only the shops on Anderson Street were still open as he sped past, but even they were closing. Everyone was home with their fires going and their doors tightly closed against the cold.

Jimmy shivered. They'd had sleet just a few days ago, and a bitter northerly wind had been whistling through Melbourne ever since. He was now more than an hour late home and he slid around the corner to his street, spraying mud against the neighbour's picket fence. Maybe Mum would be inside, warm by the stove, and there'd be a tasty stew bubbling away.

But no. As he reached the gate, a pale shape rushed out from his front door.

'James Edward Miller! Where have you been? I've been worried to death!'

Mum's face was even paler than her dress, if that were possible. Her hair fell in tangles around her face and her hands shook as she clutched at his arms.

'I've been doing deliveries, Mum,' Jimmy said firmly. He'd learned early to be steady and strong with her, to calm her down quickly and reassure her that he was fine. He'd heard people say he was 'the man of the family' now, and at first he'd thought they were stupid, but now he understood. Mum was fine if everything was as usual. It was doubt and worry that undid her.

He wheeled the bicycle through the gate and up the side, leaning it against the wall, and grabbed the paper bags out of his basket to put them on the fire. Then he realised he still had the potatoes, too. No way old man Brown was getting them back now. He took them into Mum; she was in the kitchen cooking by the light of a kerosene lamp.

'Look,' he said. 'Here's my pay.' He held out the potatoes, as well as the shilling and the sixpence that gleamed in his hand.

She gaped at the coins. 'Where did you get those? It's not payday.' She gave him a sharp look.

'You haven't been stealing like those boys from the other side of the railway line, have you?'

Jimmy gaped at her accusation. 'No, Mum. I did some extra deliveries, that's why I'm late. Not everyone pays as lousy as Mr Brown. Anyway, what's for tea? I could eat a horse.' He shoved the coins back into his pocket. He didn't want her asking exactly who had paid him, and he wanted to avoid the subject of Mr Brown tonight. He'd get out after school tomorrow and find another job, and then he'd tell her.

Just as Mum was about to answer, a loud knocking at the front door echoed through the house.

'Who on earth could that be?' Mum said, then the colour drained from her face and she staggered, grabbing at a chair, and then collapsing onto it. 'Oh, maybe it's . . . '

Mum thought every knock at the door was someone coming to tell her Arthur was dead.

'No, Mum, it's not, I'm sure.' Jimmy raced

to the door, his heart pounding. Maybe he was wrong, maybe it was someone from the Army. He opened the door.

Standing there on the front step was their local policeman, Sergeant Ross.

Jimmy sucked in a breath. Were they sending policemen with the bad news now? Was Mum right?

2

'Jimmy, I want a word,' Sergeant Ross said. 'Where's your mum?'

'In the kitchen,' Jimmy replied. 'She thought it was someone coming with bad news about Arthur.' He swallowed hard. 'You're not, are you?'

'No, lad. Sorry if I upset your mother.' Sergeant Ross paused, staring down at him. 'A little bird told me you might've run an errand for Bill Prosser earlier tonight.'

Jimmy opened and closed his mouth a couple of times before he could squeak, 'Just taking something to Mrs Prosser for him. He said it wasn't bookies' chits.'

'Pfft. And you believed him?' Sergeant Ross frowned.

'Sergeant, is Jimmy in trouble?'

Jimmy jumped. He hadn't heard Mum come down the hallway behind him.

'No, Mrs Miller. I just needed to ask him a question.' He lifted his gaze from Jimmy to Mum and his face softened. 'I hope you're well.'

'Oh, yes, so-so.'

'Have you heard from Arthur?'

'Not for a while.' Mum managed a wobbly smile. 'I'm sure he's fine. He's in Egypt, you know. Not that I understand why.'

'Training, Mrs Miller. They need our boys fighting fit and ready.' Sergeant Ross made a harumphing sound. 'I, er . . . '

Mum's cheeks turned pink. 'Jimmy, your tea's on the table, getting cold. You'd better go and eat it.'

Something was going on but Jimmy couldn't figure out what. Was Sergeant Ross going to tell Mum about his errand for Bill Prosser? He pushed the coins deeper into his pocket. He'd never forgive the policeman if Mum made him give the money back.

'It's fine, Jimmy,' said Sergeant Ross. 'Go and eat your supper, like your mother says.'

Jimmy reluctantly left them, hoping that meant the Sergeant wasn't going to dob on him. Sitting at the kitchen table, he could hear them murmuring at the front door, and then, of all things, Mum laughing!

When the door finally closed and she came back to the kitchen, her face was still pink. Jimmy had finished his stew, although there'd been too many carrots and only a few shreds of meat in it. He wiped his plate clean with a slice of bread and put the kettle on the stove to make tea.

'What did he want?' Jimmy asked.

'Nothing,' Mum said. 'Just passing the time of day.'

'But it's night-time,' Jimmy said suspiciously.

Mum didn't answer. Instead, she took a newspaper off the sideboard and laid it on the table. 'Look, Mrs Wimple next door gave me this after she'd finished with it. It says the Australians are fighting the Turks.'

'But . . . I thought Arthur was going to fight in Europe,' Jimmy said, looking at the article.

'Mr Wimple said not,' Mum said. 'He said the battalions that went to Egypt were training for this attack on the Dardanelles, and already the killed and wounded lists are being published. Arthur could be on this list – tomorrow!' Her finger stabbed the paper and her chin trembled. 'I couldn't bear it if I lost Arthur, too.'

Mum still hadn't got over Dad's death at the factory two years ago. They'd brought his mangled body home after they'd got him out of the machine, and Mum had had to manage all the funeral arrangements alone as well as grieve. What family she had lived far away in

Queensland. There were still times when she cried. Arthur obviously hadn't thought about how the constant worry might affect Mum when he'd run off to enlist.

'Nah, Arthur's too tough,' Jimmy said. 'He'll be all right.' He glanced at Arthur's postcards lined up along the mantelpiece. Egypt looked interesting with all those pyramids and funny buildings, but the desert sounded pretty hot.

'Read this!' Mum's voice grew shrill. 'It says "the glory of wounds and death incurred in their country's cause by its gallant sons". I'll bet good money it's not their son out there on the battlefield. And this bit here – "the fallen died like heroes". Heroes! To who? Not to me!'

'Mum, I keep telling you, Arthur will be home before you know it.'

But Jimmy wasn't so sure. Arthur marching off in his brand new uniform had seemed like a game, and he'd sounded so cheery in his short letters home. The newspaper reports were making the war real all of a sudden. Jimmy scanned the list of those killed. Some were from Albert Park and Hawthorn, not so far away, but lots were just slightly wounded. Maybe Arthur would be slightly wounded and they'd send him home.

Jimmy leapt up. 'Sit down, Mum, and I'll make us a cup of tea. Is there any of Mrs Wimple's butter cake left?'

'One slice,' Mum said. She sank down onto a chair and rubbed her face, leaving black streaks from the newspaper ink. 'You have it, son. I'm not hungry.'

Jimmy folded the newspaper and put it in the wood box. He'd use it to start the fire in the morning, and that way Mum couldn't read it again. There wasn't much news coming through, but what there was was too upsetting for her. He had a mind to tell Mrs Wimple not to pass on any more newspapers.

But later that night, after Mum had gone to bed, Jimmy couldn't help himself. He pulled out the newspaper again. On the next page was more about the battle, which was at the strange-sounding place Mr Wimple had mentioned to Mum – the Dardanelles. Jimmy couldn't figure out whether things were going well or not. It reported that seven hundred Turks had been captured, but 'Our Casualties Heavy'. He put the paper back in the wood box and went to bed, but it was impossible now to stop his brain from imagining Arthur lying on a beach, half a world away, blood leaking from half a dozen bullet wounds. To distract himself, Jimmy got the coins out of his pocket and lay there, flipping them over and over, making a list of all the food he was going to buy, and none of it from Mr Brown's shop! He'd go into the big shop on the corner and have a right old time.

It was a struggle to get up in the morning, but Mum roused him early and Jimmy made sure to stuff the newspaper into the fire before she saw it again. Before school, he had to chop wood, as well as polish his shoes, and then Mum sent him out with the shovel to pick up fresh horse dung in the street for the vegetable garden. He popped his coins in the tin on the mantel, worried at how little money was there.

His mum had already left for her job at the sugar factory when he set off for school at a run, and he was halfway down Stephen Street when he heard a shout.

'Jimmy! Wait up!'

Jimmy turned. It was his old mate, Frank Green. They'd had some beaut footy games in the schoolyard at lunchtime. Frank was a year older and he'd left school already so Jimmy rarely saw him now.

Frank ran up, puffing, his plump face flushed bright red. 'Why are you going to school?'

'Cause I have to, worse luck.' Jimmy knew he was terrible at everything except arithmetic.

'I thought you'd left school. Someone saw you running errands for Bill Prosser. So I thought you might be coming to work with us in the railway goods yard today.' Frank might be plump but he was solidly built and new muscles bulged under his flannel workshirt. Jimmy felt small against Frank's bulk.

'No . . . ' Jimmy said. 'Mum says I have to go to school.'

'Nah, come and work with me.' Frank grinned. 'It'll be worth three or four bob to you.'

Jimmy nearly said that just one small job for Bill had earned him a shilling, but he thought better of it. 'Why are you asking me?' he said. 'You've got plenty of mates in your gang you could ask.'

Frank shrugged. 'Thought you'd like the money. And to get out of that prison down there.' He pointed towards the school.

Jimmy shook his head, smiling. It was so tempting . . . 'I have to go to school,' he said.

'Mum'll have my guts for garters if she finds out I didn't, even if I do earn a few bob.'

'Please yourself,' Frank said, shrugging. 'Hey, what about a game of footy this arvo? Been ages since we had a kick.'

Jimmy brightened at the thought of a game of footy. Why not? He had no job at Brown's anymore. 'Yes, maybe. I'll come past your house after school.'

He watched Frank head off towards the railway yards and then trudged on to school. To be honest, he'd much rather have worked at the yards. School was so boring, and the classroom was freezing already. In the middle of winter he'd be wearing three pairs of socks and two jumpers to try and stay warm. Miss Palmerston was an old cow, and she'd been at the school so long she'd been Arthur's teacher, too. Jimmy was getting pretty sick of her telling him how much better Arthur had been, not to mention the constant raps on the knuckles with her big wooden ruler when he got his times tables wrong. It'd be nearly another year before he could leave. High school was out of the question.

Jimmy was still a couple of hundred yards from the school gate when the bell rang – two long trills. The second bell! How had he not heard the first? He was in real trouble now. Jimmy took to his heels and ran hard the rest of the way, leaping over the now-closed gate and through the front door. He clattered up the stairs, the noise echoing and bouncing off the tiled walls, and sprinted down the corridor to his classroom. All the doors were shut and he could hear the teachers in each room already droning. At the door to his classroom, he paused, tried to stop gasping like an old draughthorse, and turned the handle. It wouldn't budge.

Miss Palmerston had locked him out!

3

Jimmy couldn't believe it. The old bat! And if he waited around for morning recess, she'd give him detention or lines to write. One hundred times: *I must not be late to school.* He might as well go home – maybe he could get Mum to write a note to say he was sick. Anything was better than hanging around the draughty school corridor all morning.

As he plodded home, Jimmy thought of the shilling from Bill, and the extra sixpence. With that, he could catch the train into the city and have himself a bit of a day out. Sixpence would get him a ticket and even leave enough for an ice-cream.

No, he couldn't waste it like that. Maybe if he walked to the shops, someone would give him some errands to run. Threepence a time, that would mean . . .

Toot, toot!

Jimmy jumped – he'd been so wrapped up in his plans that he hadn't heard the motor car behind him. It was a shiny green Daimler, and Bill Prosser was behind the wheel, his hair combed back with hair tonic, a cigarette hanging from his mouth.

'Jimmy, lad! Fancy seeing you here.'

Jimmy walked around the car, admiring its big round headlights and glossy paint. 'Great car, Mr Prosser.'

'Told you, call me Bill.' Bill leaned out of the window. 'Want a ride?'

Jimmy was sorely tempted, but Sergeant Ross's words rang in his head. Gossips were everywhere around Yarraville and a ride in Bill's car would get him into trouble again. 'No, thanks.'

'Shouldn't you be in school?' Bill winked. 'Having a day off, eh? Used to do it meself all the time.'

'I was going to see if anyone wanted jobs doing,' Jimmy said.

'Good lad,' Bill said. 'Gotta help your mum. Listen, I can get you a job at the railway yards. Just for the day, like. Hop in, I'll take you over there.'

The railway yards again. Was it fate? 'I . . . I suppose that'd be all right.' The yards would pay better than errands. Surely Mum would be happy to have a bit more money in the kitty? And Jimmy would get to ride in the shiny green car. He wasn't going to turn that down. He went around and got in, breathing in the smell of leather and engine oil.

Bill drove down Stephen Street, turned left along Murray Street past the fire station, and pulled up next to the boss's office at the railway yard. He tooted the car horn again and a huge man in overalls and a battered felt hat came out.

'What d'you want, Prosser, me old cobber?'

'George, good to see you!' Bill got out of the car and shook George's hand. They talked for a few minutes and then Bill turned to Jimmy. 'Now, this is me little mate Jimmy, and I told him you'd have a day's work for him today.'

'He's a bit young, Bill,' George said doubtfully. 'And a bit weedy.'

Jimmy straightened up and tried to look tough. 'I'm as strong as a horse. And I work hard.'

'Come on, George,' Bill said. 'You're always complaining that you're short-handed with all the men enlisting. Give the boy a go.'

George pointed to a wagon loaded with bags of wheat. 'Can you carry one of those?'

Jimmy gulped. The bags looked pretty heavy, but if he said no, that'd be the end of the job. 'I reckon I could.'

'Ha!' George laughed. 'All right, Bill, he can work for a day. After that, we'll see.'

Jimmy started to say there'd be no 'after that'

but decided to keep his mouth shut.

Bill waved and drove off, and George said, 'See those men down the other end? Go with them. Tell them George said you were to help.'

'All right, George.'

'Mr Mellon, to you, lad.'

'Yes, Mr Mellon.' Jimmy ran over to the group unloading a truck stacked with crates of vegetables and passed on what George had said.

The foreman, an older man with grey hair and beard, sighed. 'I wish George would give me workers who aren't still wearing nappies. All right, get up on the back and help the other boy with those bags of carrots.'

Jimmy climbed up and discovered the other boy was Frank Green.

'Hey, how come you changed your mind?' Frank asked.

'No school today,' Jimmy said with a grin.

Frank laughed. 'Bonza. I could do with a hand. These bags are heavy.'

Together they hauled down more than twenty bags, grabbing two corners of a sack each and swinging it across to the men on the rail wagon. By the time they'd finished, Jimmy's arms and shoulders were aching, and it wasn't even time for a smoko break. Next they carried crates of cabbages, and at last the hooter went for smoko.

'Glad it's not raining today,' Frank said as they trudged over to the station building and hunkered down against the wall. Frank pulled a squashed bag of lollies out of his pocket and offered Jimmy one.

'Peppermint rock – ta!' he said. He hadn't had lollies for ages. He looked up at the grey sky as he sucked. 'Do you work in the rain?'

'Yep. Rain, hail or shine.' Frank looked up. 'Here's the rest of the gang. Hey, you lot all know Jimmy Miller?'

A dusty, ragged group of boys gathered around them, hands in pockets. The biggest one spat on the ground. 'You related to Arthur

Miller who played for Footscray?'

'Yep,' Jimmy replied. 'He's my brother. He's a soldier in Egypt, although Mum thinks he's in that Dardanelles place now, because of what the newspaper said.'

The big boy puffed out his chest. 'I'll be joining up any day.'

'Yeah, sure you will, Hector,' another boy said with a guffaw. 'You're still two years short.'

'He's always skiting about enlisting,' Frank muttered. 'Watch out for him, he's Bill Prosser's cousin. Thinks he's the ant's pants.'

'I know some who've got in and they were only sixteen,' Hector said.

'Yeah,' Frank said, 'but they're bigger than you and they can tell better fibs.'

The boys all fell about laughing. Hector looked annoyed. The hooter sounded and they all went back to work. The next loading job wasn't so bad – boxes of tinned meat – and after the lunch break, during which Frank shared a corned beef sandwich with Jimmy, they were sent into the goods shed to stack boxes and sweep the floor. It was a long day and relief swept over Jimmy when the final hooter went, but the four shillings George gave him almost made up for the aches and pains.

'You did all right,' George said. 'Good lad.'

'Coming with us for a drink?' Frank asked as they headed out to the street.

'What? A beer?' Jimmy said. Surely no one would serve them a beer in the pub.

'Nah, sometimes we get a bottle of lemonade and go down the flats for a game of footy.'

Now that was more like it. Jimmy couldn't remember the last time he'd had a decent game of footy. There were so many kids at school now that there wasn't enough room to run and kick. 'Sure will.'

As they walked past the shops and along Stephen Street, towards the paddocks, one of the boys pulled a football out of his work bag.

They kicked it all the way there, running after it when it went into people's front gardens or verandahs. A couple of times housewives came running out, shouting, 'Be off with you, you larrikins!' and the boys just laughed and whistled. Jimmy laughed as hard as the rest of them, feeling free as a bird as they raced along.

In the paddocks, Frank and Hector picked teams. Frank chose Jimmy first. 'He'll be no use to you,' Hector sneered. 'Too short and weak. Looks nothing like his brother.'

Jimmy's face burned. He was small. He longed to be as good as Arthur, but that was never going to happen. Not unless he magically grew.

'You wait and see,' Frank said, tapping the side of his nose. 'Sometimes the smallest are the toughest.' Jimmy puffed out his chest a bit and glared at Hector, pleased Frank had stuck up for him.

With teams chosen and goal posts set out with sticks, the game began. They had to dodge weeds and rocks and cows, but Jimmy didn't care. He shouted and whooped and whistled as loud as the rest of them, kicking and running and jostling for the ball until he was breathless. Hector was a mean player and several boys, including Jimmy, ended up face-first in the dirt. But Jimmy got his own back once at least, giving Hector a good thump when they went up for a mark that sent him staggering. The other boys laughed and cheered.

'Not so weak now, hey?' Frank yelled.

After one particularly good kick, another boy, George, said, 'You've got a darned good boot on you, Jim.'

Jimmy tried not to grin, but deep down he was pleased. What if he could play for Footscray one day, like Arthur? Arthur was big and tough and good-looking enough that all the girls went to watch him play. Next to that, Jimmy had always felt like one of the spindly dandelions growing in the paddock. But these boys didn't seem to think that. 'Kick it here!' they called, and 'Nice mark, Jimmy!' and they jostled him for the ball, laughing and shoving.

By the time the game was over it was nearly dark, but Jimmy was in no hurry to get home. Mum would be wondering where he was, but he wasn't keen to face her. He dawdled along with Frank, yelling 'See you!' and 'Not if I see you first!' to the others and laughing.

'You coming down the yards tomorrow?' Frank asked.

'Nah, I'll have to go to school or Mum will be spitting blood,' Jimmy said. 'Gee, I hate school though.' He knew what would be waiting for him tomorrow – Miss Palmerston would have organised one of the male teachers to give him six of the best with the strap if he couldn't get Mum to write him a note.

'Don't go,' Frank said. 'Come and work in the yards and earn good money.'

Jimmy badly wanted to, but Mum was dead

36

keen on school, always telling him how Dad would've wanted him to finish and get a good job. Besides, the law said he had to go until he was fourteen. Suddenly, it hit him – he'd been playing footy and forgotten all about the money in his pocket from the yard. What if it'd fallen out? The sweat on his skin turned icy cold and he hardly dared put his hand in his pocket to check.

Phew! The coins were still there. The relief was so great he felt dizzy for a moment.

At his street corner, he waved to Frank and headed home.

Mum was in the kitchen, slicing bread. 'Where have you been?' she said sharply. 'Why weren't you at school today?'

'I was late.' Jimmy hung his head. 'Miss Palmerston locked me out.' He dug his hand into his pocket and pulled out the four shillings, putting it on the table.

'What's that? You haven't been working for

that Bill Prosser, have you?'

'No, Mum. I worked a few hours down at the railway yards.' He held out his hands, showing her the dirt and blisters. 'See?'

All at once, she flopped down onto a chair, her head in her hands. 'Jimmy, you can't just skip school like this. I get worried sick, and the last thing I need is another visit from the coppers. I can't afford to be fined for you playing truant.' She looked up, frowning. 'And what on earth have you done to your clothes? You're filthy.'

'I'm sorry, Mum,' Jimmy said. 'Truly. I'll go to school tomorrow. Can you . . . can you write me a note? Otherwise I'll get the strap.'

She sighed. 'I suppose so. But I won't do it for you again, you hear?'

Relief flooded through him. Mr Wagstaff hit hard – last time Jimmy had been unable to stop himself from crying, and his hand had hurt for days. He raced through his jobs, feeding their three chooks and watering the garden, chopping wood for the stove and then helping Mum fill the tin tub with hot water so he could have a bath. She made him scrub all over, even behind his ears. His blisters stung in the hot water and his arms and shoulders ached, but it was a good ache, especially knowing he'd now earned an extra four shillings for the household.

The next morning, thanks to the note from Mum, Miss Palmerston grudgingly let him into her classroom without a punishment for being away. But she was still grumpy with him all day. After school, Jimmy went into every shop on Anderson Street, looking for work, but they all said no. One man glared at him and muttered something about 'Prosser . . . thieving . . . ' but Jimmy didn't dare ask him what he meant. Surely Bill hadn't put the mozz on him?

Jimmy trudged back up the street, pushing his bicycle. He didn't want a stupid shop job anyway. But now he'd have to admit the truth about losing his job with Mr Brown, and Mum would be really unhappy with him. What other work could he do? The railway yards were no good – it was all day, every day, except Sundays.

He propped his bicycle against the pole outside the grocery store and went inside to the counter filled with jars of lollies. His favourite was licorice, and this place had the long curly sticks he loved. He stared at the jars, his mouth watering so badly that he could hardly swallow. Finally, the woman behind the counter snapped, 'You buying or not, boy?' and he decided to go home and face Mum with the bad news.

The gas man was already out, lighting all the street lamps. Jimmy reached his front gate, and as he put his bicycle down the sideway he heard crying. Was that Mum? Had she found out already he'd lost his delivery job? He ran inside to find Mum sitting at the kitchen table, bawling her eyes out, while Mrs Wimple patted her hand

and poured her a cup of hot tea.

'Oh Jimmy,' Mrs Wimple said. 'Thank the Lord you're home. Your poor mother has had some terrible news.'

That meant just one thing. Jimmy couldn't speak – he stared at Mum and waited with his heart thumping like an army drum for her to tell him that Arthur was dead.

Mum stopped crying long enough to drink some tea, and then she saw Jimmy.

'Oh, Jimmy, I've had a letter.'

A letter? Was that how it happened? He thought of Arthur, marching off to war, proud as punch in his new uniform and hat, his boots so shiny they gleamed like polished copper. Was Arthur shot, or was he blown up with a shell?

Jimmy's throat felt like it had an enormous hot rock stuck in it.

'Arthur, he . . . he's been badly wounded. They don't say what that means. But . . . ' She managed a watery smile. 'He's coming home.'

'Oh.' All the air rushed out of Jimmy and he

grabbed the back of the kitchen chair to steady himself. Arthur wasn't blown up after all. He was still alive. He was coming home!

'That's beaut, Mum.' He frowned. 'So why are you crying so much?'

Mrs Wimple grimaced. 'My fault, I'm afraid. I brought the Sydney newspaper with me – my sister sent it down. It's got a photo of the wounded coming home on the ship.'

Jimmy glanced down at the newspaper lying on the table. One of the soldiers only had one leg and hobbled along with a crutch; the other's head was all bandaged up and he was being carried by another soldier. No wonder Mum was upset.

'Er, Mrs Wimple, would you mind not bringing the papers over anymore,' Jimmy said as politely as he could. 'Mum really takes them to heart.'

'Of course, I understand.' Mrs Wimple stood up. 'I've brought you a shepherd's pie for your dinner. I hope you enjoy it.'

'Thanks.' Jimmy waited until Mrs Wimple had left, then threw the paper into the fire. He poured Mum another cup of tea. 'You all right, Mum?'

'Yes, love,' she said. 'It was just a bit of a shock, that's all. I thought . . . I thought they were writing to tell me he was dead. That's what set me off.'

'Let's have some pie then,' Jimmy said. He planned to tell Mum about losing his job after dinner, but she was drooping with exhaustion and could hardly finish what was on her plate. He offered to do the dishes and sent her off to bed. Arthur might've been joking when he'd said Jimmy would have to be the man of the house, but he'd been pretty close to the mark. If only Arthur could see him now, doing every job in sight. Jimmy sighed – he still had to put the chooks away and chop some wood.

In the morning it was more jobs, and a hasty plate of half-cold porridge. Mum had gone to work, looking washed-out as though she'd hardly slept, and he forgot to keep an eye on the kitchen clock. He'd be late again, and no note this time to save him.

Instead of locking him out, Miss Palmerston was waiting for him. 'Don't bother with your excuses, James Miller,' she said. 'You were skiving off.' The other kids snickered but she silenced them with a glare.

Now, that wasn't fair. Jimmy knew plenty who skipped school whenever they felt like it, and he wasn't one of them. 'I wasn't, Miss. I was – ' Oh, what was the point. She never believed him.

She puffed up like a bullfrog. 'Don't answer me back! You can take yourself down the corridor to Mr Wagstaff, right now. Tell him to give you six, and don't come back until it's done. That might teach you to be on time.'

Jimmy ducked his head and trailed out of the room. He got halfway to Mr Wagstaff's office and stopped. Why should he go willingly to get the strap? It was totally unfair and mean and, darn it, he wouldn't go, so there!

He stuck his shoulders back and marched out of the school, back up the street and into his house. He sat at the kitchen table for a few minutes, amazed at his own daring, but the house felt too quiet, so he went out the back and started cleaning up the yard, scooping up chook poo and putting it in a bucket for the garden. He hadn't been at it long when someone hailed him from the back door, giving him such a fright he dropped the shovel.

It was Mr Wimple. He was the manager in the office where Mum worked. 'I was about to send down to the school for you, lad. Come and see to your mother, will you?'

Jimmy ran inside to find Mrs Wimple helping Mum into bed. 'What's wrong with her?' Jimmy asked frantically.

'Shhh.' Mrs Wimple tucked the covers around

Mum and pulled Jimmy into the hallway. 'She fainted in the office. She's not well at all, I'm afraid. This business with Arthur is too much for her.' Mrs Wimple patted Jimmy's shoulder. 'Will you be all right to look after her?'

'Yes. Thank you.'

When the Wimples left, Jimmy paced the hallway, peeping in at Mum now and then. She was so pale and sweaty – he got a damp cloth and wiped her face but it didn't seem to do much good. Finally, he decided to walk up and ask for the doctor to come and visit. It would cost a bit, but he was too worried about Mum.

Dr Wells had patients all morning but he agreed to come at lunchtime, and Jimmy went home to finish the backyard clean-up, popping in every now and then to check on Mum. He made her a cup of tea but she didn't touch it.

At lunchtime, Dr Wells arrived and spent some time examining her. Then he motioned for Jimmy to follow him to the kitchen.

'She has a bad cold coming on,' he said. 'However, I'm worried it will develop into pneumonia and go to her lungs. She's very rundown. Has she been eating?'

'Yes,' Jimmy said, 'but she's been worried to death about Arthur, and yesterday she got a letter saying he's been injured.'

'Oh dear,' Dr Wells said. 'Worry is just going to make it all worse.' He pulled out his doctor's pad and scribbled on it, tore the page out and gave it to Jimmy. 'Take this to the pharmacy and get them to make up the tonic and the cold remedy as soon as they can. Now, she needs to stay in bed for at least a week, maybe more if she doesn't improve.'

'All right.' Jimmy paid the doctor and saw him out the door, then he sat down on the floor in the hallway. What could he do? If Mum didn't go to work, she wouldn't get paid, and the medicine would use up what was left of the money he'd earned. They might have enough in the jam tin in the kitchen for groceries for a while, but the rent was due next Monday and the landlord had shouted at Mum once before for being short ten shillings. It'd probably be a few weeks yet before Arthur came home, but if he was injured, it wasn't likely he could work either.

Jimmy cycled up to the shops for the medicine and Mum woke up enough to drink some tea and eat a slice of toast, then he persuaded her to take the remedy and tonic. Judging by the way she screwed up her face, neither of them tasted too good. He'd searched the kitchen high and low for money but there was less than a pound in the tin and a couple of shillings in Mum's purse. The rent, he knew, was twenty-five shillings, and there was very little food in the larder.

A shilling would buy them a loaf of bread and a quart of milk. They had potatoes and a few cabbages in the garden, but butter was too expensive, and so was meat. Jimmy's stomach groaned. Why had he eaten all that pie last night?

He should've saved some.

He didn't dare ask Mum what to do. The doctor had said quite clearly that she wasn't to be worried with anything.

By the next morning, Jimmy had made up his mind. There'd be no more school for a while. He set off for the railway goods yard to ask for a job.

5

George Mellon was reluctant to take Jimmy on. 'It's lumber today. It's heavy work, lad, and I'm not sure you're big enough for it. Those other boys have got a bit more beef on them.'

'I can do it, Mr Mellon, please give me a go,' Jimmy pleaded.

'Well . . . all right. I can pay you five shillings a day, but you have to work a full day, no shirking.'

'Thanks very much. That'll do me,' Jimmy said, 'but is there any way you can pay me on Friday, please? Mum's pretty sick and the rent will be due.'

George hummed and hawed. 'All right, just this once.'

Phew! Jimmy had the rent covered now, and they would eat for the next week as well as be able to pay for more medicine, if needed. He marched down to the crew loading the wagon, feeling very pleased with himself.

The foreman, Bert, put him straight onto the wagon where they were stacking lengths of timber. Frank gave him a punch in the arm. 'Didn't think I'd see you back.'

'Mum's sick,' Jimmy said, 'and Arthur's been wounded. He's coming home.'

'That's bonzer news!' Frank said.

Jimmy frowned. 'Depends how bad he is.'

'He'll be fine,' Frank said. 'Probably just a stray bullet or he fell in a trench and broke his ankle.'

'Yeah.'

Bert yelled, 'You two, stop yer gabbing and get working!'

Frank whacked Jimmy on the back and they both set to, carrying the heavy lengths of wood and stacking them against the wagon sides. As he worked, Jimmy couldn't help thinking about how much trouble his family was in. When Arthur had insisted on enlisting, he'd told Mum his army wages would be twice what he was earning at Ebelings as a wheelwright repairing carriage and cart wheels, but Arthur had never sent a penny of it home. The nights were so cold now, and Jimmy had chopped the last of the firewood. They certainly couldn't afford coal – he'd have to scrounge around the streets for scrap wood.

By the end of the day, Jimmy was so tired and sore he could hardly walk home, let alone go for a game of footy. He trudged home alone, the early dusk making the streets gloomy. Head down, hands in pockets, he didn't see Bill Prosser standing at the door to the pub, glass in hand.

'Long day, Jimmy,' Bill said. 'You look tuckered out.'

'I am,' Jimmy said. 'But I'll have to get used

to it, I suppose.'

'I heard your mum was ill.' Bill pursed his mouth and whistled. 'Makes it hard on a good lad like you. I could do with a bit of help in me business now and then. You could earn yourself a few extra shillings, no heavy lifting.'

Jimmy tried to raise a smile but he was too tired. 'I'll be in enough trouble with Mum when she finds out I'm not at school. Sorry, Bill, I have to say no.'

'Fair enough. But if you change your mind, you know where I am.' Bill gave him a wink and went back into the pub.

When Jimmy reached home, the first thing he did was check on Mum, but she was nowhere to be seen. He called out but there was no answer, so he ran through the house and found the back door open. He felt sick in the stomach – something was wrong. Sure enough, he found Mum outside lying in a heap at the bottom of the steps.

'Mum!' He knelt next to her and raised her head off the ground.

She stirred, and her eyelids fluttered. 'Jimmy? Where were you?'

'Working, Mum.' Might as well tell the truth.

'That's nice.' She coughed, and her chest rattled alarmingly. 'I was going out to the lavatory, and I felt woozy on the way back.'

Mum was shivering, and Jimmy realised she was only wearing her underwear and slip. His face burned with embarrassment, but it was more important that he got her back to bed, and there was no way he could carry her.

'Come on, Mum. You have to get up and try to walk.'

Finally, he got her to her feet, and she slowly made her way down the hallway, leaning heavily on Jimmy. She half-fell into bed and he pulled the covers over her. 'I'll make you a cuppa, Mum, all right?'

She murmured something, and he raced off

to put the kettle on, but the fire in the stove had died out and he had to light it all over again. The house was freezing, but he soon got a roaring fire going, pushing more wood into the stove. What if Mum got worse? What if nothing he did helped? They'd put him in a children's home or an orphanage! No, Mum had to get better. He'd do whatever it took.

When the kettle had boiled, he made Mum a cup of tea with plenty of sugar, and found the old metal cylinder she used to heat the bed, filled it with boiling water and wrapped an old towel around it. That would soon warm her up.

He was starving but there was only a half loaf of stale bread left and a pot of plum jam in the cupboard. A jam sandwich would have to do.

Mum had drunk some of the tea, and she was awake when he went in to check on her. She smiled at him weakly. 'Jimmy, love, I'm sorry to be such a bother.'

He was astonished. 'You're not a bother,

Mum. I'm just looking after you like Arthur told me to.'

Too late, he realised he shouldn't have mentioned Arthur's name. Her face fell and there were tears in her eyes. 'What's he going to be like when he comes home? Some of the soldiers' wounds are terrible, they say.'

'We're not going to listen to whoever *they* are,' Jimmy said. 'Now, I'll get you more tea and you have to take this medicine. And I'll get you something to eat, all right?'

She managed a smile. 'All right, boss.'

'Don't you be giving me any cheek, now, lass,' Jimmy joked, and was happy to see her laugh. He ran all the way to the shops and had to pay a whole shilling for a mutton pie but he figured she needed building up. Sure enough, when she'd eaten some of the pie, a bit of colour came back into her face. But although she was fast asleep in no time, her breathing was shallow and hoarse, and she kept coughing. Jimmy knew he had to work at the yards again tomorrow, but leaving Mum alone again all day worried him sick. He decided to go next door and ask Mrs Wimple for help.

'Of course, Jimmy,' said Mrs Wimple. 'Give me the spare key and I'll pop in every couple of hours.'

Such a wave of relief washed over him that he could barely stand. 'Thanks, Mrs Wimple.'

He was so tired by the time he got home that he ate Mum's leftover pie without heating it up again, then borrowed her alarm clock, giving it a good wind-up and setting it for six o'clock. That way he knew he'd get to work on time.

The next day, a bitter wind blew through the yards, bringing with it flurries of hail and cold rain. They were all soaked through by lunchtime. Jimmy ran home to check on Mum, who was sleeping, ate some bread and the last of the pie, and found Arthur's old oilskin coat to wear, even though it was too big for him. The men laughed at him when he returned, but when it rained half an hour later, they were all offering him money for it.

'No thanks,' Jimmy said. 'Arthur will need it when he comes home.'

'When's he arriving?' Frank asked.

'No idea.' Jimmy straightened from the sack of sugar he'd been carrying, stretching his aching back. 'The letter didn't say. It didn't say much of anything really. The last letter we had from Arthur was just before they sailed for Gallipoli. That was months ago.'

'My mum and sister have been making up billy cans for the soldiers,' Frank said. 'They've knitted that many socks, and done packets of tea and biscuits, and they pack them all in with gumleaves. They said the soldiers put the leaves on their cooking fires, and the smell reminds them of home.'

Jimmy tried to imagine Arthur throwing gumleaves on a fire, thousands of miles away, and wearing socks knitted by Frank's mum. It made him feel a bit better.

When work finished at four o'clock, Frank asked if Jimmy was coming to play football later.

'I'd better get home to Mum,' Jimmy said. 'She's pretty sick and the doctor is worried about pneumonia.'

'We're going to the lolly shop first,' Frank said. 'You come too and I'll shout you.' Jimmy couldn't say no to that, and he promised to pay Frank back when he had some money.

The boys all crowded around the counter, arguing over which were the best lollies.

'I'm getting toffees,' George said.

'Humbugs are better,' Frank said. 'They last longer. What do you reckon, Jimmy?'

Jimmy stared at the row of jars, his mouth watering. 'Musk sticks.'

'Musk sticks?' Hector jeered. 'Only girls eat musk sticks.'

'Don't worry about him,' Frank said. 'Musk sticks it is. Here, has your mum ever had one of these Violet Crumble bars? My mum loves them.' And Frank cheerfully bought one for Jimmy to take home to Mum. 'That'll make her better in no time.'

Jimmy couldn't help thinking what a good mate Frank was turning out to be.

They said goodbye at the corner of Jimmy's street and he went into his house nervously, hoping he wouldn't find Mum passed out again in her underwear! But Mrs Wimple was there, feeding Mum some soup.

'Plenty on the stove for you, when you're hungry,' Mrs Wimple said.

Jimmy found a fresh loaf of bread waiting for him on the table, as well as a bowl and spoon all ready for the soup bubbling away. Mrs Wimple was the best neighbour in the world!

He was halfway through his second bowl when she came and sat down with him, her face worried. 'I don't like the sound of your mother's chest,' she said. 'If it's not better in the morning, I think we should get the doctor back.'

Jimmy glanced up at the jam tin and a chill ran through him. Was there even enough in the tin to pay for another visit? What choice did he have?

She stood to leave, and Jimmy said, 'Hang on, Mrs Wimple, I'll go and get you some eggs. You've been a lifesaver.' One hen was off the lay, but hopefully there'd be eggs there.

'You don't have to do that,' she said, but she looked very pleased when Jimmy brought her two warm brown eggs straight from the nest. 'Are you working at the railway yards?' she asked.

'Yes. We badly need the money.' He looked at her anxiously. 'You won't report me, will you?'

'Good Lord, no,' she said. 'But you keep an

eye out for the truancy man. If he comes while I'm here, I'll explain for you.'

'Thanks, that's beaut of you,' Jimmy said, but he had a horrible feeling that wouldn't be the end of it.

6

Even after another doctor's visit and more medicine, it was a week before Mum was well enough to sit up in the kitchen. Jimmy was grateful every day for the yards work that paid for her treatment and kept them in bread and milk.

Mum had been too ill at first to understand that Jimmy wasn't at school, but finally, when he arrived home from the yards one afternoon, she said, 'You haven't been going to school, have you?'

'No, Mum.' He stared down at his boots with their broken, knotted laces. He waited for her to scold him.

'Mrs Wimple tells me you've been working with the men, earning a wage.' Her voice was so sad that he looked up in surprise. 'It's all right, son, I understand. I wish you were at school, but we have to eat and pay the bills. No use crying about it, I suppose.'

'It'll be back to normal soon,' Jimmy said. 'The war will be over and Arthur will be working and you'll be as right as rain.'

She sighed. 'We got a letter today,' she said. 'From Arthur. Months old, of course, but . . . ' She pointed to the mantel where the letter stood against the clock.

Jimmy opened the envelope, his heart racing. The writing was rough and hurried, the paper thin, but he read slowly, deciphering as he went.

Dear Mum and Jimmy,

Well, we've been in this place for over a month now, and the heat is starting to set in. The flies are getting worse, too — they make the Australian bush fly look like nothing. They crawl on everything, including the dead and wounded, and get into our food. More than once I've eaten a fly by accident. It'd usually turn my stomach good and proper, but I hardly worry about it these days.

Jimmy, you'd be thinking we were all rabbits the way we've had to burrow in here. We dug ourselves into the sides of the hills, and there are more trenches further up where the fighting is. The Turks are also in trenches, closer than we'd like. Their snipers are a damn nuisance, even having a go at the ones who go swimming in the sea.

Mum, I stink to high heaven. I'm sure you'd be telling me to have a bath!

We're all keeping each other's spirits up, but it's hard. Not long ago we had an armistice for a few hours, so everyone could bury their dead. I'm sure you don't want to hear any more about that.

I miss your cooking, Mum. Bully beef every day for every meal isn't too good!

Love to you both,
Arthur

Jimmy looked up. 'What does he mean about burying the dead? I thought we were winning.'

'I don't know,' Mum said. 'The newspapers have been making it all sound very heroic, but the letters they publish from the soldiers are more honest, I think. The numbers of dead and wounded just keep growing.'

'So when is Arthur arriving? Why won't they tell us?'

Reading Arthur's letter was like hearing his voice, and it reminded Jimmy of all the fun they'd had – Arthur teaching him how to ride the bicycle, the day their old rooster had sat on Arthur's head and pooped on him, watching Arthur play footy. Arthur was so proud when he got his job at Ebelings – would they take him back?

Jimmy just wanted his brother home again,

not burying rotting bodies on a hill on the other side of the world.

'Mrs Wimple gave me the newspaper today,' Mum said. 'Look at this.'

Jimmy hoped this newspaper would have better news. Sure enough, it said there was a hospital ship heading their way with two hundred Victorian soldiers on board. It was landing in Western Australia that day, and then coming to Port Melbourne via Adelaide.

'He could be here in a week!' Jimmy said.

'That's right,' Mum said, smiling. 'I really have to get my health back. And you can help me clean out Arthur's bedroom.'

Soon after, there was a knock on the door, and when Jimmy opened it, there were Frank and George, asking him to come out for a game of footy. Now Mum was feeling so much better, Jimmy decided to go.

They walked together along Anderson Street, right to the end and out into the paddocks. All around green oats were growing but a couple of paddocks were laying fallow, and on one of these the game had already started. Jimmy and his mates joined in, playing with the other boys from the yards and a bunch of boys from the school in Powell Street.

Jimmy kicked off his old boots and felt like he was flying as he leapt for the ball and ran and kicked. It'd been cold all day, and now as the boys played, their breath puffed out in white gusts, then a light drizzle started and the dirt in the paddock turned to sticky mud. Clods of it stuck to their boots and it felt like thick socks on Jimmy's bare feet.

Hector was playing with his usual shoving and thumping, but a couple of the bigger boys from Powell Street soon gave him as good as they got, and Hector ended up on his bum in the mud. Jimmy couldn't help laughing and Hector's face darkened into a scowl.

Uh oh, Jimmy thought.

Sure enough, a few minutes later, Jimmy had the ball and was about to kick it when Hector came running towards him, teeth bared. Jimmy got rid of the ball quick smart, but Hector didn't pull up, barrelling into Jimmy and knocking him a few feet onto his back. He lay there, half-winded, and Hector cackled. 'Not so funny now, ya little sissy.'

'Hey, no need for that,' Frank shouted, but Hector ignored him and ran off.

Jimmy staggered to his feet. If only he was big and tough like Arthur, he'd give Hector a good thumping. One day . . .

When it got too dark to see the ball, they all agreed the score was even, and the boys headed off home for their supper. Frank and Jimmy scraped the mud off their feet and Jimmy carried his boots under his arm as they walked back along Anderson Street.

'Is your brother going to be on that ship next week?' Frank asked.

'We hope so. Why?'

'They're planning a big parade – they reckon every soldier coming back will ride in a car through the city.' Frank wiped his face on his sleeve. 'They asked Mr Willis next door to take his car and be part of it – so I said I'd wash and polish it.'

'I'll help,' Jimmy said. He could just see Arthur sitting like a king in the back of Mr Willis's Daimler, waving to the crowds. He and Frank agreed that he would go to the Willises' house after work next Tuesday and make sure the car sparkled.

Jimmy couldn't wait for Arthur to arrive, and the week dragged, especially because they spent a lot of the time in the yards loading and unloading coal and coke. It was a dirty job and Jimmy went home covered in black coal dust every night. Mum would make him stand out in the backyard until she could tip a bucket of warm water over him, then he'd run inside and hop in the tin tub to scrub himself clean. He had more baths in that one week than he'd had in a year!

At least with the regular money they were eating better. Jimmy was usually starving by the time he got home at night.

On Tuesday evening, Jimmy and Frank cleaned and polished the Daimler from headlights to back number plate, until it gleamed. Mr Willis beamed under his big moustache. 'You boys have done a first-class job. She looks like a brand new car.' He offered to give Jimmy and Mum a ride to the docks at Port Melbourne, and Jimmy gratefully said yes. Otherwise they'd have to go by train and tram, and walk a fair way, too. Mum was much better, but that'd tucker her right out.

On Wednesday, Mr Mellon allowed Jimmy to leave work early, and it was just as well. Mum took some persuading to get into the Daimler – she'd never ridden in a car before! Mr Willis had the top up as rain was forecast, and they were at the docks in no time. The ship had just berthed, and as they watched, the men on the wharf set up the gangplank.

Jimmy didn't know who was more nervous, but it was probably Mum. Dozens of soldiers lined the rails of the ship, and they were searching for family on the docks as desperately as those below were looking for a dear, familiar face. Ever so slowly, soldiers started to walk down the gangplank, many with bandages around their heads or arms in slings. As they were recognised by those waiting, there were shouts and cries of joy.

'I can't see him, Jimmy!' Mum said, tears trickling down her face.

'He'll be there, Mum, don't worry,' Jimmy said, but he was worried now. He'd searched along the rails three times and there wasn't a sign of Arthur. Maybe he wasn't on this ship after all. A sigh went up through the crowd, and his gaze whipped back to the gangplank. All the soldiers who could walk on their own had disembarked – now it was the turn of those who needed help.

Jimmy's mouth dropped open as several soldiers with legs missing and makeshift crutches came down leaning heavily on mates or nurses dressed in white. One soldier with an arm and a leg missing was even being piggy-backed. Then came several soldiers who shuffled along, blank-faced, as if they had no idea where they were. A woman cried out and ran to one of them, hugging him, but still he seemed not to realise he was home, let alone who she was.

Mum shuddered, her handkerchief to her mouth. 'Oh Jimmy,' she said, 'this is just too awful to bear.'

But worse was to come.

Another soldier stood at the top of the gangplank, head down, leaning on crutches, with an enormous bandage around his head, covering one eye. His right leg was missing, his trouser leg pinned above his knee. He appeared to be stuck there, unable to move forward until a nurse came and murmured in his ear. She moved in closer and put her arm around his waist, urging him onto the gangplank, and finally he gripped the crutches and took a faltering step.

Jimmy watched, frozen, as they inched downwards. Surely this couldn't be . . . but it was. It was Arthur. Mum realised just after Jimmy, and rushed to the bottom to wait for him; Jimmy followed slowly, his heart banging against his ribs. Where was the muscled footy player who'd marched off last year?

As Arthur reached the dock at long last, he looked up and saw Mum waiting. She ran forward and threw her arms around him, sobbing, and Arthur was forced to stand there. Jimmy realised that if Arthur put his arms around Mum, he'd probably fall over, as the nurse had moved away to help someone else. Mr Willis was nowhere in sight, so Jimmy moved to Arthur's good side and waited for Mum to stop crying.

Arthur patted her on the back as best he could. 'Mum, stop, please. We need to move out of the way.'

Finally, Mum nodded and blew her nose. 'I'm so glad you're home, Arthur. I'm sorry, I just . . . '

'I know,' was all Arthur said, but it was enough. Then he spotted Jimmy. 'Jeez, mate, you've shot up like a gum tree!'

Jimmy tried to grin. 'I've been eating your share while you were gone.'

'Good on you.'

Jimmy spotted Mr Willis waiting not far away. 'Listen, Arthur, there's going to be a big parade. All you blokes are being driven through the city – it's a big welcome home. Mr Willis has brought his Daimler and – '

'No.' Arthur looked around and Mr Willis came over straightaway. 'I know you all mean well,' Arthur said to him, 'but I can't face it. And I'm not going to the hospital either. I've had enough of all that. I just want to get home, and I reckon a lot of the others will feel the same.'

'Fair enough,' Mr Willis said. 'You're the heroes – what you say goes.'

Arthur laughed bitterly. 'Heroes? No bloody way.'

Mr Willis pursed his mouth but he didn't reply. He led the way to his car and they drove back to Yarraville in silence. He helped Arthur out of the car and said, 'If you need anything at all, just let me know. I mean it.'

'Thanks,' Arthur said, and hobbled inside without another word.

'I can't thank you enough,' Mum said. 'I'm sorry you missed the parade.'

Mr Willis pulled out a hanky and wiped his forehead before putting his hat back on. 'That's all right. I didn't realise how bad they'd be, so many of them. It was a bit of a shock.'

Not half as much as it was for us, Jimmy thought. He followed Mum inside and found

Arthur sitting on his bed, his face ghostly white and sweaty.

'I'll put the kettle on for a cup of tea,' Mum said. 'I've made a cake, too. Your favourite, Arthur, apple cake with custard.'

Jimmy knew Mum had made it with suet instead of butter, and the last of the wormy apples from their tree, but it still smelled good.

'I'd love a decent cup of tea, Mum,' Arthur said, finally showing a bit of enthusiasm.

Jimmy didn't know how to get his brother up on his crutches again, but the promise of tea and cake got Arthur moving, awkwardly and with a couple of groans of pain. He made it as far as a kitchen chair before collapsing again with a big thump. He had to grab the table to stay upright.

'Sorry,' he said, grimacing. 'Didn't get much chance to practise with these useless things on the ship.'

Mum poured the tea and sat opposite Arthur,

examining him closely. 'Will your head wound need dressing?'

'It's not my head, Mum,' Arthur said roughly. 'It's my eye. It's gone, like my bloody leg.'

Mum paled and pressed her lips together, then she said, 'But you're home, son, and you're alive, and that's all I care about.'

'I'm no good to anyone like this,' Arthur barked. 'I might as well be dead.'

'Don't you dare say that!' Tears brimmed in Mum's eyes again, but she blinked them back and began cutting the apple cake. She put a big slice in a bowl for Arthur and poured the custard over the top. 'There you go. Jimmy, how about a piece for you? You boys did a lovely job on Mr Willis's car.'

'Thanks, Mum,' Jimmy said quietly. He ate his cake and custard but each mouthful seemed to stick in his throat and it took several swallows and two cups of tea to make it go down. Every now and then he sneaked a glance at Arthur, who seemed to be having just as much trouble eating his own cake. He'd lost so much weight that his face looked sunken in.

Jimmy had been looking forward to Arthur coming home for so long, and now it was nothing like he imagined. Arthur wasn't the same person who'd gone marching off, hat at a jaunty angle, face shining with pride. This Arthur was bitter and angry. He'd left all his pride at Gallipoli.

7

Supper was quiet that night. Arthur had agreed to move into the front room, and seemed grateful for the opportunity to get out of his uniform and into the normal clothes he'd left behind. Mum had washed and ironed everything, patched and mended where necessary, and used some of their not-really-spare money to buy Arthur new socks and underpants.

Jimmy fed the chooks while Mum made soup, and then helped her with the dishes. Arthur had gone off to his room as soon as he'd finished eating, and when Mum went to look in on him, she came back and said he was fast asleep. 'It's not going to be easy for him,' she sighed.

Jimmy voiced what had been ringing in his head all evening. 'Arthur's right, Mum. How's he going to get a job like that?'

Mum had no answer for him. Jimmy went to bed early – it was hard to make himself get up so early in the freezing mornings, let alone if he hadn't had enough sleep. When he woke, it was pitch-black and he couldn't see the clock, then he realised what had woken him. Someone was shouting at the top of his voice. Who was making that racket?

Jimmy jumped out of bed, felt his way to the door and opened it to find Mum rushing past with a flickering candle. He followed her into Arthur's room. On the bed, Arthur writhed and thrashed, his good leg twisted in the sheet. 'No, no!' he shouted. 'They're firing again! Duck! Get in the trench!'

Mum put down the candle and knelt next to the bed, trying to soothe Arthur or wake him, but he flung out an arm. 'Get 'em off me. There's maggots in my shirt. Get that dead Turk out of here. Fix bayonets! Charge!'

Mum fell backwards onto the floor and Jimmy rushed to help her up. 'You'll have to help me,' she said. 'Hold his arm while I try to wake him.'

Arthur had always been much stronger than Jimmy, but Jimmy's work in the yards had made a big difference. He was actually getting muscles like Frank. All the same, he was astonished at how thin Arthur was now, and how easy it was to hold him down. Mum ended up slapping Arthur gently on his hand and saying sharply, 'Arthur! Wake up! You're home now. Wake up!'

Finally Arthur's eyes opened and he blinked, dazed. 'Mum? Am I really home?' But when Mum tried to comfort him, he pushed her away. 'Leave me alone.'

Arthur huddled in his bed and cried great ragged sobs, as if his whole world had crashed down on him, and it had. His shoulders heaved and Jimmy listened helplessly, feeling as though he was being torn apart inside. Arthur was so changed that it was hard to remember what he'd been like before.

Mum seemed to understand, and she took Jimmy back to his room. 'We'll have to be patient with him,' she said, 'and give him time to heal, inside and out.'

'How much time?' Jimmy asked. 'What if he's always like this?'

'We have to believe he'll get better,' Mum said. 'Then maybe he will, too.'

Jimmy went back to bed but he got little sleep for the rest of the night. Although Arthur didn't shout and scream again, he did mutter and groan on and off, and when Jimmy got up for work in the early dawn, he thought his eyes might drop out of his head. Down at the yards, Bert was in a bad mood and shouted at the boys every five minutes.

'You lot, stop gossiping like old women! We've got ten wagons of superphosphate to load this morning!'

Jimmy hated loading the heavy bags of fertiliser. It stunk, and if a bag had even a small hole in it, the stuff spilled out and made him sneeze. By lunchtime, they still had four wagons to go and Bert made them work through until they were done. That was when Jimmy realised that he'd come without anything to eat, and he was too tired to walk home for a sandwich.

'Where's your lunch?' Frank asked. Without waiting for an answer, he handed Jimmy half of his huge doorstop sandwich. The thick slices were a bit stale but the bacon and egg inside were like food from heaven.

'Mmm, thanks, mate,' Jimmy said, his mouth full.

Frank worked on his own sandwich for a few minutes, frowning and staring off into the distance before he finally asked, 'So, how's your brother?'

Jimmy shook his head. 'Not good. He kept us

up all night with terrible dreams and shouting, and he acts like he doesn't even want to be home.'

'Mum said when the soldiers came back from the Boer War, they took ages to get used to being home again.' Frank sniffed and wiped his nose on his sleeve. 'Her brother never really came right again.'

'He didn't have any bits missing, though, did he?'

'No, but he never got married. Said he wouldn't want any girl stupid enough to have him.'

'So what happened to him?' Jimmy finished the sandwich and wished he had another.

'He went off into the outback somewhere to look for gold. Mum hasn't heard from him for years.'

'Oy, you two!' Bert was shouting from the end of the platform at the station, waving them over. They ran over to see what he wanted, and he gave them two big brooms. 'Give the platforms a good sweep. People are complaining that the fertiliser has been blowing this way from the wagons.'

Once they'd finished that job, Bert let them stop for the day. 'Hop over and see Mr Mellon. He'll give you your pay.'

'But it's only Friday,' Frank said. 'We usually get paid on Saturday.'

'No work for you tomorrow,' Bert said. 'Come back Monday.'

Frank shrugged and was happy to get his money and have a day off, but Jimmy wasn't pleased at all. That was five shillings he'd be short this week, and Mum still wasn't back at the sugar works office. He wasn't looking forward to telling her.

'How about we meet tomorrow afternoon and go to the footy,' Frank said. 'Melbourne is playing Carlton in the semi-final. We can catch the train into the city and walk to the ground.'

Jimmy's face lit up. He hadn't been to the

footy for ages – not since Arthur had enlisted. 'That'd be beaut.' Then he stopped. 'Except . . . I need to check with Mum first. With Arthur, you know . . . ' And would there even be any money spare for a train ticket and then entrance to the game?

'Yeah, I know,' Frank said. 'How about I meet you on the corner by the pub around lunchtime, and we'll see then if you can come.'

'All right.'

Jimmy had great plans about asking Mum that evening, but after he'd collected his pay and walked home, he found Sergeant Ross knocking on the door.

'Good timing,' the policeman said. 'I was coming to see your mum about a few things.'

'Yeah?' Jimmy made a face behind Ross's back. Didn't they have enough to worry about? Mum came to the door and invited Sergeant Ross in for a cup of tea, and when they got to the kitchen, Arthur was sitting there by the stove, hunched over his cup.

'Arthur, good to see you home again,' Ross said in a fake hearty voice that made Jimmy cringe.

'Is it?' Arthur growled.

'Now, Arthur,' Mum said, her face pink. She took the cake tin off the shelf and cut the last of the apple cake into small pieces, offering them to the policeman. He took one and bit into it. 'Mmm, lovely.'

Jimmy didn't sit down. He took his cup and stood at the back door, watching the chooks pecking in the backyard while he waited to find out what Ross wanted. He had a fair idea and, sure enough, it didn't take long to get to it.

'I've had a report from the school that Jimmy hasn't been attending. Is he sick?'

Jimmy swung around, ready to tell Sergeant Ross what he thought of him, but Mum's glare pulled him up. 'I can't afford for Jimmy to be at school. He's a fine boy and he's got himself a job down at the goods yard. His wages are all that's keeping us right now.'

'You've lost your job?' the sergeant asked, his eyebrows raised.

'I've been quite ill,' Mum said. 'There's no wages for me when I'm not working, not like some. So I'll thank you to tell the school that Jimmy will be back when we can manage it, and until then, if they want to take us to court, good luck to them!'

Jimmy stared at Mum, hiding a grin behind his hand. He'd never heard Mum be so tough before. And he sure was glad that Sergeant Ross couldn't make him go to school, but now he felt doubly bad about losing a day's pay. After the sergeant finished his tea and cake and left, promising to let the school know, Jimmy faced his mum.

'This is all I got paid this week,' he said. 'I'm really sorry but they just said no work again until Monday.'

'That's all right,' Mum said. 'We'll manage. I should be able to go back to the sugar works very soon, I hope.' She glanced at Arthur as she said it, but he sat in silence, staring at nothing, as if he hadn't heard a word.

Jimmy didn't mention the footy game – instead he went out the back and fed the three chooks, and collected three eggs.

'You girls are like a little egg factory,' he said. He shooed them into the big shed and latched the door, and as he was carrying the eggs inside, an idea struck him. What if they had six chooks instead of three? There was plenty of food out in the paddocks he could get for them, and maybe he could ask the neighbours for food scraps. If he sold a few dozen eggs, then he could afford a bag of feed for them. Maybe Arthur could even take over their care and egg collecting when he was better.

He bounded inside to tell Mum his idea.

'Hmm. Let's look at it in the spring,' she said.

'Any chooks you bought now would still be having their winter break from laying, I think, or be too young.'

'All right.' Jimmy sighed. He hadn't even got as far as mentioning Arthur's role.

Mum made scones to go with their soup that night, and they all retired early to save on the kerosene lamps, but again, Mum and Jimmy were woken by Arthur's nightmares, and this time Arthur thrashed around so much that he fell out of bed with a terrible crash. At least it woke him up, but he needed their help to get back up again.

'I'm sorry, I'm sorry,' he gasped. A sob escaped, although clearly he was trying very hard not to cry.

'You have to give yourself time,' Mum said. 'Would it help to talk about it? Tell me what happened?'

'No!' Arthur turned away from her. 'Just leave me alone.'

Mum hesitated but Jimmy took her arm and pulled her gently away. 'Mum, come on.' He led her to the kitchen and made them both a cup of tea. She sat at the table, her face white and drawn, her hands shaking.

'It nearly kills me to see him like this,' she said. 'It's so terrible. And there's nothing we can do.'

Jimmy drank his tea in silence. He didn't know what to do either, but he knew one thing – he couldn't gallivant off to the footy tomorrow acting like he didn't have a care in the world and leave Mum to cope alone. He'd do his jobs in the morning and then meet Frank and give him the bad news.

8

When they met the next day, Frank wasn't upset with him at all, and said he wouldn't go either. 'But if it was Fitzroy playing, you couldn't have kept me away.'

'Fitzroy? Fancy barracking for a useless team like that!' Jimmy laughed, knowing Frank wouldn't take offence. He'd taken plenty of teasing from Frank over his support for Footscray, who weren't even in the League. 'Maybe we can watch Fitzroy play next week.'

'You're on,' Frank said. 'Let's go and buy some licorice and then find the boys.'

Sure enough, two of Frank's mates, Walter and Freddie, were out in the paddock with a footy. The four of them kicked it around for a bit, but without enough boys for a game they soon grew bored.

'I know where there's an apple tree hanging over the back lane,' Walter said. 'I reckon they're fair game.'

They followed him through the back streets and into the laneway, but the tree had already been stripped bare. The boys trudged along and around the corner, and found Old Cobbley's horse and cart waiting patiently in the street.

'Let's play a trick on him,' Freddie said.

'He's delivering vegetables,' Jimmy said. 'He'll be out any minute.'

'Nah,' Frank said. 'He lives here. He's having lunch before he finishes his deliveries. If we're quick . . . ' He scooted around to the front of the horse and started unbuckling the harness. 'Quick, give me a hand.'

Freddie ran around the other side and did the same, and then, while Jimmy held the cart shafts,

Walter led the horse through the gate into the front garden. Frank and Jimmy quickly fed the shafts through the fence pickets, and Walter tied them back on the horse. In a few minutes, there stood the horse on one side of the fence and the cart on the other, all harnessed up again.

The boys ran off and hid around the corner, poking each other and snorting with laughter. Not long after, Old Mr Cobbley came out of his house and exploded. 'What nasty little rats did this?' he roared. 'If I get a hold of you, you'll wish you'd never been born!'

The boys were laughing so hard now they could barely stand, and they had to stagger off down the street before their merriment gave them away.

'Oh my golly gosh,' Frank said, holding his stomach. 'That was a classic.'

'It's past two o'clock,' Walter said. 'What about going to the pictures this afternoon?'

'Let's see what's on first,' Frank said. They

wandered up the main street and across the railway line, then turned right to the St George theatre. The films showing had been written up on a blackboard.

'Oh, it's Charlie Chaplin,' Frank said. 'At least he's funny, not like that Mary Pickford, the soppy "sweetheart".' He wrapped his arms around himself and mimed someone giving big smooching kisses. 'Mmm, oooh, you're so handsome, Frederick.'

Freddie's face turned bright red and he wrestled Frank to the ground. The boys cheered and when Freddie let Frank up, he said, 'Why can't they show a film about the war? So we can see what adventures those soldiers are having. I can't wait to join up. I'm going to sneak in as soon as I turn fifteen and tell them I'm older.'

'Yeah, yeah,' Frank said. 'You haven't even got fluff on your face yet, let alone some decent whiskers. Who do you think you're fooling?'

Jimmy said nothing. It wasn't so long ago

he'd thought like Freddie and wanted to enlist like Arthur and maybe end up fighting next to him. Now it was different, and he wished he could take Freddie to see Arthur, see what really happened to soldiers.

'Look,' Walter said. 'They're going to show the film about Gallipoli next week! Hey, Jimmy, your brother should come and see it.'

'What the hell for?' Jimmy yelled. 'He's just bloody been there and got his leg blown off and his eye shot out. You think he needs a reminder?'

'All right, all right,' Walter grumbled.

'Calm down, Jimmy,' Frank said. 'It's just that the war is a long way away, and the papers make out like it's the most exciting thing ever. Join up and see the world, they say!'

Jimmy nodded and mumbled, 'Sorry.' There was no point yelling at Walter. He wasn't to know any better.

'I've gotta go and check my traps,' Freddie said. 'You coming?'

They all decided to go, walking out into the paddocks towards Geelong Road, following cow tracks that meandered and crisscrossed. Freddie knew exactly where all of his traps were. 'I've got my special spots,' he told them, 'and I know just where those bunnies like to run. I don't need a dog or a ferret.'

Sure enough, every trap but one had a rabbit in it and soon the boys were carrying two or three each. Freddie was happy to sell Jimmy a rabbit for their tea – Mum would be pleased to have fresh meat, although Jimmy wasn't looking forward to gutting and skinning it.

When he got home, Arthur was sitting by the fire, reading the newspaper and looking very gloomy. Mum was writing a letter and glanced up as Jimmy came in, holding the rabbit proudly out in front of him.

'Where did you get that?' she asked.

'Off Freddie – he's a mate from the goods yard. He's got traps everywhere.'

Mum fetched a sharp knife from the drawer. 'That'll be lovely for our tea. Now, Arthur, why don't you give Jimmy a hand with getting it ready?'

Arthur grunted something and Jimmy thought he was going to refuse, but he pulled himself to his feet and grabbed his crutches. 'Best we do it in the backyard.'

Jimmy had skinned and cleaned a rabbit several times before, but he was happy that Arthur was going to help. However, all Arthur did was lean against the back porch and criticise. 'You need to cut further down than that' and 'Don't pull the guts out like that'.

Jimmy gritted his teeth and kept going, but he ended up making a bit of a mess of it, all thanks to Arthur, who took the rabbit in to Mum. Jimmy heard him say, 'Sorry it's all cut up. Jimmy's not much good at this. You'd think he'd know by now. Has he been a lazy begger since I've been away?'

Jimmy was so angry his hands were shaking. Why did Arthur have to be such a mongrel? He didn't wait to hear what Mum said. He buried the rabbit guts and went to the tap for a bucket of water to clean off the back steps before finding an old frame in the shed for the rabbit skin. He washed the blood off and then stretched the skin over the frame and scraped it clean of fat and tissue. After it dried he'd hopefully be able to tan it. A couple of rabbit skins would make nice warm glove liners for Mum.

It was dark by the time he finished up, so he put the chooks away and trudged back inside. The delicious smell of rabbit stew filled the kitchen, but Arthur was still there, sour-faced, so Jimmy went to his room to play with his marbles. But when he'd tipped them out of the bag, he no longer felt in the mood. He put them away, hoping Mum was right and Arthur would get better.

At least Arthur seemed to enjoy the rabbit

stew, eating seconds and thirds, leaving nothing in the pot. Mum said nothing, but usually she would've used the leftover stew and stretched it into Sunday tea for another meal. Arthur didn't seem to realise that eating the whole lot was a problem. Jimmy watched him and couldn't help worrying how much money would be left in the tin for food by the middle of next week.

The next day, Mum and Jimmy got ready for church as usual, but Arthur refused to go.

'I'm not hobbling down there just for them to stare and gossip about me. Besides, it's pretty clear God has given up on me.'

'Arthur!' Mum's mouth was a thin line. 'If God had given up, you'd be lying under the dirt at Gallipoli, not home safe and . . . ' Too late, she'd been about to say safe and sound, and sound was something Arthur was not.

He just shook his head and stomped off to his

room, his crutch clattering against the skirting board.

After a long boring day, Jimmy went to bed, looking forward to work the next morning just to get away from the house.

But bad news greeted him at the railway yards.

'I'm sorry, lad,' Mr Mellon said. 'I can give you work today, but from tomorrow I need strong men to cope with the heavy freight coming in. Maybe next week we'll have the lighter bags and crates again.'

'But I need the money,' Jimmy said.

'I can't pay you to sit around and watch. Why don't you try the shops up the street. Surely they're looking for delivery boys?'

Delivery work paid less than half what he'd been getting at the yards – besides, he'd already tried that. All the same, when Jimmy finished work that afternoon, he started asking around, even going to Arthur's old workplace. Everywhere he went, either the work was too hard for a boy or he needed experience.

He walked home, worry dragging his feet and weighing him down like a ton of coal. How on earth was he going to tell Mum?

Suddenly a voice hailed him from the door of the pub. 'Jimmy! How're you doing at the yards?'

It was Bill Prosser, wearing what looked like a brand-new suit with a flower in the buttonhole. His shoes shone like black glass and his shirt was as white as a wedding dress.

'Hello, Bill.' Jimmy tried to sound happy but it wasn't in him today.

'Things not good?' Bill asked. 'George not giving you a hard time down there, is he?'

'He's a good boss,' Jimmy said, 'but he reckons I'm too small for a lot of the loading. He can't give me a permanent job, only days here and there now when the freight is lighter.'

'That's a shame,' Bill said. 'How's Arthur?'

'Not good.' Jimmy grimaced as his stomach

rumbled. He'd had no lunch again that day and had refused Frank's half sandwich, feeling like a bludger.

'Here,' Bill said, reaching behind him to a table just inside the door. He presented Jimmy with a plate with a meat pie on it. 'It's a bit cold – I got talking and forgot about it. You have it.'

Normally Jimmy would have refused someone else's leavings but he was way too hungry. 'Thanks.' He grabbed the pie and took a huge bite, gravy running down his chin. At least if he ate this now, it wouldn't matter if Arthur scoffed everything at home.

'You know, I wish you would come and work for me,' Bill said. 'I know you're trustworthy. And you're a hard worker, aren't you?'

'I am,' he replied cautiously.

Bill leaned down close to Jimmy and tapped the side of his nose. 'It'd be between you and me and the gatepost. No one else needs to know.'

Bill's smile warmed Jimmy like a comfy blanket.

'Sergeant Ross knows everything around here,' Jimmy said.

'No, he just likes to think he does,' Bill said. 'Ross does all right on the small stuff, like chasing up truant kids and throwing drunks out of the pub, but he stays out of my business. If you came to work for me, I can guarantee you won't hear a word from the copper. Not one word.'

'Really?' Still, Jimmy hesitated. He was already in trouble for truancy. What if he ended up in gaol?

'Look, I'll pay you the same as the yards — five bob a day — plus bonuses for special jobs. No heavy lifting, but your bicycle will come in handy. Can't say better than that.'

Bill sipped his beer, his eyes shifting left and right as he waited for Jimmy's answer.

Jimmy couldn't help it — he looked over his shoulder in case Sergeant Ross was coming up behind him, but the coast was clear. It was risky even talking to Bill. But Jimmy knew he had no job, a near-empty jam tin at home, and an injured brother to feed who wasn't likely to get any kind of work either. Bill was offering good money. Surely the risk was worth it?

Jimmy finished off the pie, chewing while he pretended to think about Bill's offer, but he already knew he'd say yes.

'Sounds like a fair deal,' he finally said.

Bill stuck out his hand. 'We'll shake on it, then. A man's handshake is as good as a contract, right?'

Jimmy nodded. His hand, calloused and rough, felt trapped by Bill's strong, smooth grip, but it was too late to back out now. Besides, he needed the money – that's all there was to it.

'Righto, I'll need you at eight sharp tomorrow. Come to Mum's house, around to the back door.'

'I'll be there,' Jimmy said, and set off for

home. One minute he wanted to kick up his heels and skip, the next a dark sense of dread slid through him. He almost wished he could just go back to school and play with his marbles in the schoolyard again. But then he remembered Arthur, and Mum's worried face, and the empty money tin, and knew he had no choice.

The next morning he had no need to rise early for the goods yard, but still Jimmy was up before seven, stoking the fire for Mum and filling the kettle. He set the porridge on to cook and went to let the chooks out, shivering at the nip in the air. Time to go before Mum saw him.

Jimmy made sure he put on his good shirt and jumper, and cleaned his boots with a brush and rag. After breakfast, he wheeled his bicycle out to the street and set off for Somerville Road, arriving at Mrs Prosser's back door well before eight o'clock. Rather than knock and maybe interrupt their breakfast, he sat on the step and waited. When he heard a mantel clock inside chime the hour, he stood and rapped on the door.

Bill answered it. 'You're right on time, Jimmy. I like to be punctual myself. You're off to a good start.' He took a parcel off the shelf by the door. 'Here's your first job – take this to the post office for Mum. Here's sixpence to pay for it.'

Jimmy was a little taken aback. He'd expected to be doing something illegal, but maybe Bill was testing him. He put the parcel in his bicycle basket, rode to the post office and was back in less than half an hour, only to find that Bill had gone out. Mrs Prosser told him to spend the morning weeding her vegetable garden, and Bill would be back later.

Indeed he was and, after a bowl of soup and some bread for lunch, he took Jimmy out in his car. 'I want to show you where to go,' he said. 'You'll need to know all the ins and outs before you start. I can't be spending all my time explaining stuff.' They drove around the streets of Yarraville and Footscray, past the fertiliser factories, the abattoir, the sawmill and the tanneries. At each one, Bill pointed out the main gate and the side entrances. 'When you come here,' he said, 'you wait by that entrance and the men will come out to you. On no account do you ever go inside, even if they ask you to. You got that?'

'Yeah, but what am I doing?'

'Taking bets. You gotta problem with that?' Bill's voice was sharp.

Jimmy shook his head. 'Where will you be?'

'Nowhere near you,' Bill said with a short laugh. 'I've got a few places I might be. The pub later in the day, or my own place.'

'I thought you . . . '

'Lived with Mum?' Bill laughed again. 'Not likely. She'd cramp my style.' He pulled up outside a large brick house not far from Seddon railway station. 'This is my place. But you never come in the front door, right? There's a back lane and a gate – you come in there so your bicycle is off the street, out of sight, and knock three times. Can you remember all that?'

'Yep,' Jimmy said, and shivered. What went on at Bill's house? It had bars on all the windows, and the back gate looked like a fortress. Bill was showing him secret things that might get him in deep trouble if he wasn't careful. He straightened his shoulders. Well, in for a penny, in for a pound. 'Yes, Bill. I won't let you down.'

'Good lad.' Bill clapped him on the shoulder. They drove back to Somerville Road and Jimmy collected his bicycle. He rode home slowly, lost in thought, and nearly toppled off into the gutter when a voice boomed in his ear.

'Where've you been?'

It was Frank, grinning like a monkey, covered in dust and mud from the yards. He had his football tucked under his arm.

'Working,' Jimmy said. He was reluctant to tell anyone, even Frank, what his new job was.

'Where?' Frank didn't beat around the bush.

'Er . . . for Bill Prosser.' Jimmy's face reddened. 'But don't tell anyone.'

'Don't worry, I'll keep my trap shut,' Frank said. 'But watch yourself. Bill's got a finger in lots of pies. The bookie business is only part of it. And watch Hector, too.'

'What for?'

'Hector's always skiting about how he's going to work for Bill one day. He won't like it that you got in before him.' Frank looked over his shoulder. 'Look, here come the others. We're off for a kick down the paddock. You coming?'

'Yeah, that'd be great. I'll see you there,' Jimmy said, grinning. He rode on home and found Arthur on his own in the kitchen.

'Where have you been?' Arthur said. 'Mum needs more wood for the stove.'

Jimmy glanced at the wood bag beside the back door. It would've taken Arthur only a few minutes to sling the bag over his shoulder and fetch a couple of pieces of wood himself. Jimmy was about to say so when he noticed Arthur's white, sweaty face and shaking hands.

'Are you all right?' Jimmy asked.

'Of course I'm not!' Arthur snapped, then sucked in a shuddering breath. 'Sorry, Jimmy. I just . . . the pain in my head is giving me hell today.' He went to pick up the cup of tea in front of him but his hand was shaking too much and the tea slopped across the table. 'Ahh, for the love of . . .'

'I'll fix it.' Jimmy grabbed the dishcloth and mopped up the tea. 'You want a fresh cup?'

'Yeah, thanks.' Arthur sat, hunched, staring at the table. He looked like an old man, older even than Dad had been when he'd died. Jimmy tried to conjure up a memory of Arthur in his football kit, face shining after a good game, but this weak, defeated Arthur in front of him made it impossible.

Jimmy brought in some wood and stoked the fire, then he put the kettle on. The big pot held a delicious-smelling soup that set his stomach rumbling. He eyed Arthur and wondered whether to tell him about the new job, but decided against it. Even Mum needed to be kept in the dark, as she'd probably make him chuck it in.

The front door opened and an icy gust swirled down the hallway to the kitchen. Mum came in, pulling her knitted hat off and unwinding a scarf. 'It's so cold out there tonight,' she said. 'Set the table, will you, Jimmy?' She took a parcel out of her bag and set it down by Arthur's elbow. 'Here you are. Take some now and more before you go to bed.'

'Thanks, Mum.' Arthur managed a crooked smile.

'And I bought a bandage and dressing for your eye,' she said. 'No argument, Arthur. I'm cleaning it after dinner and putting the new dressing on.'

That was one thing Jimmy didn't want to see,

but after they'd eaten and washed the dishes, Mum asked him to help, fetching soap and warm water in a bowl and holding a towel ready. It took ages for her to peel the old dressing off, and Jimmy's dinner rolled and churned in his stomach as he watched. What would Arthur's missing eye look like? Would it be all bloody and full of pus? He swallowed hard and tried to look as though he wasn't worried at all.

Mum had to soak the dressing, which was stained reddish-brown and smelled like old meat, and dirty water ran down the side of Arthur's face.

'Hold the towel under his chin,' Mum ordered, and winced as she pulled the last bit away. Arthur sat like a statue, not making a sound, but his teeth ground together. Instead of a hole, his eyelid had healed almost closed, and the surrounding skin was a combination of pink mostly healed scars and one raw patch.

'There,' Mum said. 'Fresh air will do it good.

I'll dab on some of this ointment and cover it up again. You should be able to go without a dressing in a couple of days.'

Arthur nodded but said nothing, and when Mum had finished, he said goodnight and went off to his room. Jimmy sank down onto a chair. 'Phew. I was expecting . . . I dunno.'

Mum smiled. 'It would've been healed by now but he scratched it again in his sleep last night.' She rinsed out the bowl and washed her hands again before sitting down with Jimmy. 'I'm worried about him. He's . . . not right, and I don't know what to do about it. If only your dad was here.'

'Can Arthur get a wooden leg?' Jimmy asked.

'I don't know,' Mum said. 'I hope so, if it means he can move around more. It's not good for him to sit inside here all day, every day. I'm not sure he could get any kind of job on crutches either.'

'What sort of job could he get with one leg

and one eye?' Jimmy muttered.

Mum didn't have an answer for that. 'I'm hoping he'll be well enough that I can go back to work this week. I've just been down to the factory. They said they'll give my job to someone else soon if I don't.'

Jimmy sat in silence. The way things were going, he was doomed to work for Bill forever, and where would that lead? Probably straight to gaol. All he could do was hope Bill stuck to simple tasks and left him out of the really dangerous stuff.

The next day, Bill sent him out on his bicycle as a runner around the factories and tanneries, taking bets and running messages. He had a leather pouch hidden under his shirt and it was soon bulging and heavy, filled with paper and money. By the time he pedalled home that night, he was exhausted. He reckoned he must have done about twenty miles or more. Just as well Yarraville and Footscray didn't have many hills. There was no way he'd have any energy for footy if this kept up.

The day after that, he arrived at Bill's house to find a pretty red-haired young woman out in the backyard, hanging washing on the line. Jimmy felt his face flush red at the sight of the lacy drawers and petticoats hanging in the weak sunlight.

'Hello,' the young woman said, smiling. 'You must be Jimmy. I'm Lola. Isn't it lovely to see the first day of spring?'

'Hello,' Jimmy mumbled, keeping his eyes down.

'Bill said you'd help me tidy up and move furniture this morning. Do you mind?'

'No.' Jimmy was relieved. His legs were aching from the hours on his bicycle the day before.

Inside, Lola led him to a large room filled with chairs, a table, a dresser and some boxes. 'We need to move all this out,' she said, 'so I can sweep and clean, then put the chairs back.'

Jimmy didn't ask questions, he just did as Lola directed. She made him a cup of tea and a sandwich for lunch, but the tea was weak and the bread was stale and dry. Cooking obviously wasn't one of her skills.

Bill turned up when all the work was done and inspected the room. 'Good, good,' he said. 'Now, Jimmy, I need a hand tonight. You up for an extra few bob?'

'Sure,' Jimmy said, hoping it didn't mean more cycling.

'Be here by eight,' Bill said, and sent him on his way.

Jimmy couldn't think what to tell Mum, short of a lie. But the Wimples next door had invited them all over for tea and a game of cards, and Mum was cheerfully ironing her good dress. Even Arthur had agreed to go, to keep Mum happy, and when the card game started it was easy enough for Jimmy to excuse himself and pretend he was going home. He put a couple of pillows in his bed to make it look like he'd had an early night, hopped on his bicycle and was soon at Bill's house.

'Where's your coat, Jimmy?' Bill said.

'I don't have one.' Jimmy's old coat for wearing to school and church was too small for him now, so he usually wore two jumpers when it was cold.

Bill rummaged around in a cupboard by the back door and pulled out a moth-eaten tweed jacket. 'Here. It'll be too big for you but that doesn't matter.' He watched Jimmy put it on and laughed. 'You look like my granddad. Never mind. I want you to stand by the back gate with the bar across it and let people in. No one's allowed in without the password. It's "first day of spring". That was Lola's idea.'

'All right,' Jimmy said. 'How many are coming through?'

'About a dozen,' Bill said. His mouth thinned

and his tone was steely. 'But if the coppers turn up, make sure the bar is right across the gate. Then you come running in, quick smart, to let me know. Got it?'

Jimmy nodded, but his stomach was twisting in knots. Lola came into the kitchen with a rag and some penny coins and started polishing them up. That meant just one thing – a two-up game! He went out in the backyard and waited by the locked gate. Within a few minutes there was a sharp knock and a man murmured on the other side, 'First day of spring.'

Jimmy let him in and the man brushed past without even looking at him. He was soon followed by several more, and after about twenty minutes Jimmy had counted fourteen had gone into the house. He was dying for a pee, and opened the gate to check the lane was empty, then closed it and put the bar down before rushing to use the dunny in the corner of the yard. The hours stretched out. It was boring standing out in the cold but he didn't dare nick off home without Bill's permission. The only entertainment was watching the men stagger out to the dunny and back in again, each one even drunker as the night went on.

At last they had all left through the back gate again, and Bill came out, smoking a cigar. 'Ah, what a night,' he said. 'You did a great job, Jimmy. Here's your bonus.' Bill handed him two half-crowns. 'I'll give you a lift home. You can get your bicycle tomorrow.'

Jimmy wasn't about to argue. His eyes felt like they were falling out of his head, and he was dozing off in the car before they were halfway back to Yarraville.

Bill let him off at the corner and he crept into his house, suddenly realising when he heard the clock chime that it was well after midnight. All he wanted to do was drop into bed and sleep, but as he sat on the edge and bent to take his boots off, something moved under the covers and his heart nearly leapt out of his chest.

'James Miller,' Mum said, sitting up in his bed. 'Where have you been?'

10

Jimmy had to wait for his heart to slow down from a gallop before he could answer. 'I've been working, Mum.'

'The goods yard doesn't operate at this time of night. What's going on?'

'I've got another job,' Jimmy mumbled.

'Doing what?' She shook his arm. 'Enough of the sidestepping, son. We'll have no lies in this house.'

Jimmy sighed. Mum put honesty above everything else, including money. He didn't like his chances but it was time to front up. 'I'm working for Bill Prosser, Mum. They put me off at the yards 'cause I'm too small, and I haven't been able to find anything else.'

Mum's hand flew to her mouth in dismay. 'Oh Jimmy, anything but that.'

'I've got no choice!' Jimmy cried. 'I tried everywhere. They all say I'm too young, but they don't seem to give a toss that we've not got enough food to put on the table!' He took the coins from his pocket and pushed them into Mum's hand. 'Here – this is for tonight. We need to eat, Mum, and pay the bills, and I'm the only one can earn a living right now.'

'Shhhh,' Mum said. 'Don't let Arthur hear you talk like that. He's upset enough about not working as it is.'

'Well, it's true!' Jimmy squared his shoulders. 'I'm sorry Arthur is in such a bad way, Mum, but if I have to look after us all, I will. I'm going to keep working for Bill, just for a while, until we get back on our feet. Then I'll stop, I promise. But if you make me stop now, and then you lose your job, we'll starve. We might even lose the house, and that's a fact.'

Mum sat in silence for a long time and then she let out a huge sigh. 'All right, just for a while. But if Sergeant Ross comes calling, we mustn't say a word about it, all right?'

Jimmy thought Sergeant Ross only came calling at their house to see Mum, but he said nothing. He didn't want the copper to be quizzing him about anything, and he planned to make himself scarce if Ross came around. Mum went off to bed and Jimmy was asleep in seconds, still in his clothes and Bill's tatty jacket.

The next morning, Mum insisted on giving the jacket a clean and mending the cuffs and collar before Jimmy took it back. Bill didn't even notice – he shoved it back in the cupboard without looking at it and said, 'Let's get cracking. I've got several jobs for you today.'

It meant more cycling around the factories, but not as far this time, and his last errand was to the butcher for Mrs Prosser. When he came back with her pounds of good steak, thinking she must be having a party, she wrapped three pieces up and said, 'Here you are, lad. Take these home to your mum. Present from my Billy.'

'Gee, thanks, Mrs Prosser.' Jimmy pedalled home as fast as he could and handed the steak to Mum with a big grin. 'Here you go, get your teeth into this.'

'Steak!' Mum said. 'Golly, I can't remember the last time I saw meat like this.'

'My mouth's watering already,' Jimmy said. 'I'm off to see if the boys are playing footy – won't be long.'

By the time he got to the paddocks, the other boys had already marked out an oval and stuck some trimmed tree branches up as goal posts. There were nearly two dozen boys milling around, laughing and practising their kicking with a couple of footballs, and Jimmy recognised some from school. One, a boy called Harold, said, 'What happened to you? Miss Palmerston went looking for you outside with her paddle. You shoulda seen her face when she came back empty-handed!'

Jimmy said, 'I've got a job now. My brother's come back from the war in a bad way. Mum needs me to bring in some money.' He laughed. 'I sure don't miss Miss Palmerston!'

'Fair enough,' Harold said. 'I wish I was you. She's a right old witch.'

'Come on!' yelled Frank. 'It'll be dark soon. Let's pick teams. Jimmy, you be captain of the red team and I'll be captain of the blue.'

Jimmy beamed with pride. He'd never been captain before – maybe this was his chance to shine. Even Hector's sour face didn't put him off, although he made sure not to pick Hector for his team. Frank had a bunch of blue material strips that his players tied around their arms.

Then the game was on!

They raced around the paddock, shouting and kicking and handballing, shoving and tackling.

Frank was a good punter, but Harold on Jimmy's team was, too, and it was an exciting, evenly matched game. Any time Hector came near, Jimmy set off after the ball, finding someone to tackle to stay out of Hector's way.

'Swap ends!' Frank shouted. The goal post down one end had a big bend in it that made it easier to kick a goal, and now Jimmy's team had that advantage. Harold put one through, and Jimmy followed with a beaut of a goal that went straight through the middle and gave them the lead. Hector's face was like a storm, and a few minutes later, when the ball was heading their way, he came up behind Jimmy and pushed him hard.

Jimmy staggered but then spun around quickly and gave Hector a good shove back. Hector grunted in surprise.

'What's the matter with you?' Jimmy snapped.

'Just can't take any more of your bulldust, that's all,' Hector said. 'Bill's a fool for taking you on.'

'If you don't like it, go and tell him, not me.'

'I will, don't you worry,' Hector growled. But Jimmy knew he wouldn't dare.

'Oy,' Frank yelled, 'get on with the game!'

Jimmy spun away from Hector and made sure he kept right away from him for the rest of the game. His team was still winning, and by the time it was too dark to play anymore, they were hanging on to the lead by a whisker. Jimmy put in a last-minute kick to goal that soared high into the air and through the goal posts. Everyone cheered and some of the boys clapped him on the back as they headed for home.

'Phew!' Frank said, hands on his knees, trying to catch his breath. 'That was a darned good game, Jimmy. You're magic when you get going. Pity we don't have lights we could switch on. I could play all night.'

Jimmy glowed. No one had ever told him he was good. It was always about Arthur. He wished he was here now to see him play.

'It's spring now,' he said. 'The days are getting longer and we can play longer.'

'Yeah, but in a couple of months it'll be time for cricket.'

Jimmy nodded sadly. He wasn't keen on cricket – not like football, where you could run around all day. All that standing around on the cricket pitch with flies landing on your face and the sun burning down – no, he'd rather play footy any day.

'I'm off,' he said. 'Maybe see you tomorrow night for another game?'

'I reckon we'll be here.'

On the way home, Jimmy thought about Hector and his threat. What if Bill did listen and got rid of Jimmy? He shrugged to himself. Nothing much he could do about it. His mind went to the steak that would be waiting for him. He could almost taste it, imagine chewing it, the juices running down his chin. Yum! He scooted down the sideway and found the chooks already roosting in the henhouse, so all he had to do was latch their door. As he pulled off his boots on the back porch he smelled the meat cooking and his stomach groaned. He rushed inside.

In the kitchen, the lamp cast a yellow glow and the fire had warmed the room up nicely. Mum and Arthur sat at the table. Arthur leaned back, rubbing his stomach. 'Here he is,' he grumbled. 'Just as well we didn't wait.'

'Sorry,' Jimmy said. 'We were playing football. I got to be captain.'

'Yippee,' Arthur said bitterly.

'Here's your tea,' Mum said. She took a pot lid off the plate that had been keeping warm on the stovetop.

Jimmy stared down at the tiny piece of steak. It was hardly bigger than an egg. 'What happened to my steak? There were three huge pieces.'

'You took too long to come home,' Arthur said. 'I thought you couldn't have been too hungry, so I had some of yours.'

'What?' Jimmy gaped at Arthur in disbelief.

'Arthur does need building up,' Mum said feebly, but Jimmy could tell from her face that she'd let Arthur just go ahead and be a big pig.

Jimmy stood up, fists clenched, shaking with the desire to punch Arthur right in his greedy mouth. 'I've been working all day . . .' He sucked in a furious breath. 'Thanks for nothing!' He picked up his plate and said, 'I'll eat in my room', and left, ignoring Mum's plea to come back. He sat on the floor by his bed, the plate on his lap, and picked up a potato. But he couldn't put it in his mouth. His appetite had disappeared and all he wanted to do was throw the plate across the room.

There was a quiet knock at the door, and although he refused to say 'Come in', Mum did anyway. She sat on the bed and didn't say anything for a while, then she slid down next to him on the floor. 'Eat up, Jimmy, please.'

'I'm not hungry.' Jimmy was horrified at the shake in his voice and he clamped his teeth together.

'I know Arthur did the wrong thing,' she said.

'You should've stopped him,' Jimmy said bitterly. 'I earned us that steak.'

'Yes, you did,' Mum said. 'But we have to try to understand how Arthur's feeling. You know, he had dreams of playing for Footscray again one day. Dreams of getting married. He had a sweetheart he was writing to while he was away. He believes it's all gone, that he'll never lead any kind of life.'

Jimmy made a face. He hadn't known Arthur had a girl. 'What happened?'

'She came to see him today, but Arthur got angry and told her to go and find someone else. He shouldn't have said it, but he's convinced she just feels sorry for him now.' Mum let out a big sigh, then she nudged his arm. 'Go on, eat. It's getting cold. And Jimmy?'

'Yes, Mum?'

'I am very, very proud of you, son, and I know your dad would've been, too.' She got to her feet. 'Mrs Wimple gave me some lemon cake today, so if you eat your tea, I'll let you have as big a piece as you can find room for.'

'Thanks, Mum.' Her words meant far more to him than lemon cake. As he ate, he thought about Arthur. No, he'd never play footy again, never get to run and kick and have a great time with his mates. That'd be the worst thing, never mind about girls. He finished his tea and headed to the kitchen for what he planned would be an enormous slice of cake.

Over the next couple of weeks, Jimmy was kept busy running around for Bill, collecting money and betting slips, going to the shops for Mrs Prosser, and sometimes washing and polishing Bill's car. He was also a regular on the back gate for the two-up games, and Bill was generous with his bonuses when he thought Jimmy had done a good job. All the same, Jimmy spent those nights with big knots in his stomach, dreading the sound of police whistles as they swooped in for a raid.

Frank and the boys were always ready for a kick of the footy, but they also went rabbiting and once caught the train to Williamstown to go fishing, although they didn't catch even a sprat or two.

Mum went back to work, worried she'd lose her job otherwise, and walked home at lunchtime every day to check on Arthur.

Nothing seemed to help Jimmy's older brother. His appetite disappeared, and although Jimmy was glad to get a bigger share of food, when Arthur lost weight and started to look like a dying man again, Jimmy wished his greediness would come back. Sometimes Jimmy and Mum would sit in the kitchen after Arthur had gone to bed, trying to work out what they could do to help, but Arthur refused to talk to anyone, let alone his own family. He just muttered, 'I don't want to be reminded. Leave me alone.'

One afternoon, Lola gave Jimmy a plate of leftover roast beef slices to eat. He was sitting on the back step, wondering if he should wrap the leftovers up and take them home for Mum, when he overheard Bill talking to one of his men, Mick Murphy, just inside.

'It's on for tomorrow,' Mick said. 'Pat's coming down from Sydney today on the train and he's determined to go ahead with it. He's bringing his –'

'No,' said Bill. 'No guns. After that heist at the Railways in Sydney, I'm not risking my neck with Pat waving a revolver around. He's as likely to shoot me as anyone.'

Guns? Jimmy's stomach lurched and the meat in his mouth turned to thick chalk.

'How are you going to get them to hand over

the cash box then?' Mick asked.

'I've got a plan,' Bill said. 'Don't you worry. You just keep Pat happy, and make sure he doesn't get drunk tonight.'

Jimmy sat very still, the plate on his lap. If Bill knew Jimmy had overheard them talking about guns, he'd be pretty angry. Maybe he could sneak out the back gate and scarper.

But before Jimmy could move, Mick stepped out the door.

'Hello, hello,' he said. 'How long have you been sitting here, lad?'

Jimmy shrugged. 'Not long.'

'Yeah, I bet.' Mick stuck his head through the back doorway. 'Bill? Come here a minute.'

Jimmy felt the blood drain from his face as Bill came out, munching on a beef sandwich. 'What is it?'

Mick gestured at Jimmy. 'Your boy here was listening where he shouldn'ta been.'

'That right?' Bill glared down at Jimmy, his

eyes like slits. 'Do you know what we were talking about?'

Jimmy could hardly breathe. He managed to squeeze out, 'Not really.'

'Hmm.' Bill took another big bite of his sandwich and kept his gaze on Jimmy as he chewed and swallowed. 'Well, I'm giving you fair warning. You tell a single soul, I'll break your bloody legs, I will. You got that?'

Jimmy managed a jerky nod.

'I wanna hear you say it,' Mick growled.

'I – I'll keep quiet,' Jimmy stammered. 'I promise.'

Mick scowled and Jimmy stood up quickly to leave, but Bill said, 'Come inside, Jimmy. I've had an idea.'

Jimmy followed the two men into the house, his legs like jelly. In the two-up room, Bill pulled out three chairs and sat on one, waving the other two to sit down. 'Listen closely,' he said to Jimmy. 'You can do me a favour tomorrow. A big favour, one I won't forget. I've got a special pick-up lined up for the morning. Your job is to wait around the corner for us on your bicycle, and when I come past and throw the bag to you, you take it to an address I'm going to give you. Then go straight home.'

Jimmy couldn't breathe. This sounded like something far worse than running bookies' errands. Surely Bill wasn't serious?

'Why give the bag to him?' Mick asked.

'They'll be looking for our car,' Bill said. 'Or even my car, if the coppers suspect me. They won't be looking for a boy on a bicycle.'

Mick grinned. 'I get it. That's a cunning plan, all right.'

Jimmy thought it was the worst plan in the world. He didn't know what Bill was up to, but he knew it was something that would get him into major trouble if he got caught. And it was something that might involve guns! He started trembling and twisted his hands together tightly. If he got caught, it would mean years inside. There'd be no leniency just because he was only twelve. He could see himself already, in prison clothes, living with rats and eating porridge for breakfast, lunch and tea.

'Jimmy?'

'Huh?' He stared at Bill like a rabbit caught in a trap.

'I want you here first thing tomorrow morning. And you remember – not a word to anyone, or you'll pay for it.' Bill's face was no longer jovial and friendly. His eyes were like slate and his mouth was a mean, hard line.

Jimmy mumbled 'All right' and almost ran from the house. It took him three goes to get on his bicycle and stay upright without wobbling all over the street. To make matters worse, it had started raining, a cold, drenching drizzle, and water ran into his eyes, half-blinding him. He pedalled home as fast as he could, but the whole way Bill's words kept spinning around and around in his head until he thought he would go mad.

Broken legs, guns, you'll pay . . .

He was in big trouble, and there was no way out.

11

Outside his house, Jimmy leaned his bicycle against the verandah post and looked up and down his street. The drizzle turned everything dull and grey — the wooden houses, tin roofs, front verandahs, gravel road. He could already imagine the neighbours at their front gates, pointing at his house and whispering about 'the Miller boy in gaol'. What would Mum do? She'd die of shame.

He wouldn't help Bill, he just couldn't. But what choice did he have? Bill had the power around Yarraville to make his life a misery. If Bill gave the word, Jimmy wouldn't be able to get a job anywhere, and Mum might even lose hers. Who knew how far Bill's crim network extended? Jimmy didn't want to even think about broken legs!

He shivered and rubbed his face, then ran his fingers over his bicycle bell and gave it a gentle ting. It was one job — all he had to do was pick up a bag and deliver it. How hard could that be?

A series of loud squawks pierced through his worries. The chooks! Was there a fox in the backyard? That's all they needed, to lose the chooks and their eggs. Jimmy ran down the sideway and into the yard, pulling up short, his feet almost skidding out from under him.

There was no fox. Instead, Arthur was sitting on the ground under the big apple tree, his leg sticking out in front of him, his crutches to one side. His head was bowed and the freezing rain had soaked his shirt and trousers right through. He'd obviously been there a long time.

Jimmy's feet felt as though they were glued to the ground, but he realised that Arthur was shaking with cold and finally he managed to make himself walk across the yard.

'Arthur?'

Arthur's head jerked up and he stared at Jimmy through reddened, desperate eyes. 'Go away.' A sob burst from him. 'Go on, get the hell out of here!'

'I . . . I can't.' Jimmy swallowed hard, trying to get rid of the huge, aching lump in his throat. 'You have to come inside.' If Arthur stayed there, he'd literally catch his death of cold. Or was that what he wanted?

'No, I don't. Go, I told you. Leave me alone. I just want to stay here. Until . . . ' Arthur's voice broke and his head went down again. Another series of shudders rocked his body. The dread inside Jimmy spread, and he dropped down in front of Arthur.

'You can't do this, Arthur,' he said. 'Come on, I'll help you up.'

'No. I'm just a burden.'

'You're not, truly.' Despair washed over Jimmy. How could he talk Arthur out of this? He had no idea what to say, except maybe the truth. 'You can't do this to Mum, Arthur. You can't be so selfish and . . . nasty to her. She won't be able to go on.'

'Nasty? Ha!' Arthur scoffed. 'You have no idea what nasty is. You have no idea how it feels to be a piece of rubbish that's no use to anyone.'

'Well . . . ' Jimmy thought for a moment. 'Why don't you tell me then?'

'You wouldn't understand!'

'How do you know?' Jimmy remembered Bill's nasty expression, the threat in his voice. 'I might understand more than you think. Tell me what nasty means.'

'It doesn't mean hero, for a start.' Arthur leaned back against the tree trunk and groaned. 'The newspapers love that word – hero. It's a load of tripe. There's nothing heroic in going ashore in some godforsaken place and being shot to smithereens. There's nothing heroic about lying in trenches covered in flies and maggots. And there's nothing heroic in your mate lying dead in the stinking sun for a week so that when you go to drag him out to bury him, his rotting arm comes off in your hand.' Arthur sobbed again, his hands over his face. 'When am I ever going to stop thinking about all this? It sits inside my head, night and day, and there's no rest from it!'

Jimmy opened his mouth but nothing came out. What could he say to all that? No wonder Arthur had nightmares and screamed in his sleep. 'Maybe . . . maybe it's like when Dad died,' Jimmy said.

'What's that got to do with it?'

'When he died, and they brought him home, I sneaked in to see him, even though Mum said I wasn't allowed.' Jimmy folded his arms tight against his chest. He didn't want to remember this, but if it would help Arthur . . .

'I was at work,' Arthur said. 'I only saw him in his coffin.'

'Yeah. That was after they cleaned him up.' Jimmy took a breath. 'They put him in the front room, with a blanket over him, until the undertaker came. I dunno why. Mum said he shoulda stayed at the factory, but the owner . . . Anyway, I went and looked.' Jimmy didn't want to go on, but Arthur had stopped crying and was listening intently. 'He was all busted up. The machine must've caught more than half of him and just crunched him up. Some of his bones were sticking out.'

'Jeez, Jimmy. No, you shouldn't have looked. I'm sorry you did.'

'But that's the whole thing,' Jimmy said in a rush. 'I did see him, and for days afterwards I had nightmares. I know you thought it was just because we'd lost Dad, but Mum guessed, and she talked to me. A lot. It was like all the talking took the worst of it away, little by little, and the nightmares did stop, eventually.' Arthur didn't look convinced but Jimmy kept talking. 'I know it's nothing like what you've been through. Geez, what could ever be that horrible? I can't even imagine what it was like for you over there. But I reckon . . . I hope . . . one day it'll get better for you. It'll take a while, I know, maybe a long while. But if you let me and Mum help you, if you talk to us . . . we love you, Arthur, and we'll do anything we can.'

Arthur was silent but Jimmy had one more thing to say.

'I meant what I said, Arthur. If you got sick and died, Mum wouldn't bear it. She's already poorly. She takes things to heart, more than a lot of people do, and having you home means more to her than you know. If you died, it would be like losing Dad all over again. You can't do that to her.' Or me, he wanted to cry out, but he kept that bit back. 'Please, come inside with me.'

Arthur sucked in a long, shuddering breath

and let it out again. 'All right.'

Tears sprang into Jimmy's eyes, burning and blurring, but he blinked them back as hard as he could. 'Good-o,' he whispered.

'Come here,' Arthur said, and Jimmy launched himself into Arthur's arms, hugging as tightly as he could, and Arthur hugged back. A fierce, tight hug. There was nothing wrong with Arthur's arms.

'My bum's gone numb,' Arthur said. 'You'd better help me up.'

Jimmy put his arms around Arthur's chest, thinking it'd be near impossible to get him up, but to his surprise he was able to lift his brother fairly easily. He leaned Arthur against the tree while he got the crutches set up, then they hobbled together slowly across to the back door and into the kitchen. Jimmy got the fire roaring, leaving the stove door open, and helped Arthur out of his soaking clothes and into dry ones. By the time they'd both had a couple of cups of hot, sweet tea, Arthur had stopped shivering and a little colour had come back into his face.

He stared into the flames for a long while, then he said, 'You won't tell Mum about this, will you?'

'No, I promise.' Relief washed over Jimmy and he felt a glimmer of hope that Arthur would start improving now, but it was mixed with his dread of what was coming tomorrow with Bill.

Jimmy's mind skipped from Arthur to Bill, and he could barely eat his stew for tea. It was Bill's stew, paid for with Bill's money, and it stuck in his throat. When he went to bed, he was unable to sleep, and when Arthur had his usual nightmare, Jimmy was happy to send Mum back to bed and get up and sit with him.

In the morning, even a basin of cold water splashed over his head didn't help to liven him up. After Mum went to work, he sat at the table staring into his cup of tea.

'Jimmy.' Arthur poked him on the arm.

'What's wrong? You're not still thinking I'll –'

'No.' He checked the clock. Bill had said first thing, so he should've been on his way by now, but he couldn't move.

'Are you working for Bill today?'

'Supposed to be.' And then he'd be carted off to the lockup.

'What's going on?' Arthur peered closely at him. 'Has Bill got you doing something illegal?'

Jimmy snorted. Everything Bill did was illegal.

'I think you'd better cough it up,' Arthur said. 'Right now. I can see it's eating away at you. Come on.'

Suddenly, it burst out of Jimmy like an egg breaking and splattering all over the floor. The two-up, the collecting money, and the job that might involve guns.

Arthur listened quietly and then whistled, long and low. 'It's got to be a robbery. You've really landed yourself in a pickle.'

'I know!' Jimmy said. 'I'm not stupid. But we had no money, and Mum was going to lose her job. It was all right until this.'

Arthur rubbed the good side of his face. 'This is my fault.'

'Don't be stupid. I was the one who –'

'Didn't you ever ask yourself why Bill was so keen to take you on?' Arthur didn't wait for an answer. 'Bill's a piece of work, all right. When I was playing for Footscray, he tried to bribe me to throw a game. Had all sorts of ways worked out for me to make the team lose. He stood to make a small fortune from the betting.'

Jimmy's mouth fell open in astonishment. 'But you –'

'No, I turned him down flat. He threatened me, but I ignored him. Then I enlisted and got all caught up in the excitement of going off to fight. Never really thought about it again. Maybe I should've reported him.'

'So you reckon Bill is paying you back by

getting me doing illegal stuff, making me the patsy. Gee, he can sure hold a grudge.' Jimmy started to feel a hot spark of anger inside.

Arthur thought for a moment. 'Stay here. Don't go. Tell Bill I'm sick and I need you.'

It might work, but it might not. Besides, he couldn't hide behind Arthur forever.

The clock ticked loudly on the mantel. Bill would be looking at his fancy pocket watch by now. Mum would be sitting in her office chair, thinking everything was all right. Frank would be daydreaming about their next footy game, never thinking Jimmy might not be there to play again. It wasn't fair. He was just trying to get by.

Jimmy made up his mind. He stood up.

'I'm going to Bill's.'

12

'You can't do that!' Arthur said. 'Bill will beat you silly and toss you into the back alley.' He clacked his crutches together angrily. 'If I wasn't so damned useless, I'd deal with him for you.'

'I know,' Jimmy said. 'But I've had enough of Bill Prosser and I'm going to tell him so.'

Jimmy climbed on his bicycle, his heart thumping in his ears like an army drum, but he didn't feel like a soldier and he certainly didn't feel as brave as his words to Arthur had been. The spark had almost fizzled out. His hands shook on the handlebars and his legs felt like they were stuffed with cottonwool. All the way, he wished for a bolt of lightning to hit him, or a horse and cart to run him down, or even just for his bicycle to crash into a big mud puddle.

But none of this happened, and soon there he was, at Bill's house. A strange car sat out the front, an old Daimler with worn seats and bent mudguards.

Rather than go around the back, Jimmy knocked on the front door.

Bill opened it. 'Where have you been?' he said angrily.

'Home, having my breakfast . . . and thinking,' Jimmy said.

'I don't pay you to think,' Bill snapped. 'Get in here.'

'No, thanks,' Jimmy said. 'I just came to tell you that I won't be working for you anymore.'

'Is that right?' Bill glared at Jimmy, his face turning dark red. 'So I suppose you're going to run off to the coppers now, are you?'

Jimmy felt the angry spark ignite again and pushed his fear back down. 'No, I'm not. You know I'm not a squealer. And my brother wasn't either.'

Bill leapt forward and grabbed Jimmy around the neck, shaking him. Jimmy gasped, struggling to breathe. 'Bill, I . . . '

'You're a turncoat, Jimmy, is what you are,' Bill snarled. 'I oughta get my iron bar out right now and whack it around your legs. Two of ya on crutches – that'd make ya mother cry, wouldn't it?'

Bill's threat sent an icy chill through Jimmy's guts, but he wasn't going to back down now. He twisted and straightened in Bill's grip and stared him in the eyes.

'I'm sorry, Bill, but I can't help you. I've got Mum and Arthur to take care of. Do your worst to me, if you really have to.'

A flash of something that might've been admiration crossed Bill's face, then he shook his head and shoved Jimmy away from him. 'Get the hell out of here, then, and don't come whining to me when you need money.' He slammed the door, and Jimmy sagged, grabbing at the verandah post. He'd been half-expecting Bill to do something much worse, beat him up or take him down to the river and throw him in. He staggered down the path, climbed on his bicycle and rode home, wobbly at first and then faster and faster. The further away he got from Bill Prosser's house, the lighter he felt. He let out a 'Yahooo!' Freedom felt pretty darned good!

Arthur was waiting for him at the front door, worry etching deeper lines into his face. He broke into a cheer when he saw a grinning Jimmy racing up the street. 'By the look of you,' Arthur said, 'you're home clear.'

'Yeah, I hope so,' Jimmy said. 'He was pretty mad with me, and he thought I'd run off to tell Ross, but I won't, even though I know I should.'

'If Ross is any kind of copper,' Arthur said, 'he'll catch Bill without our help.' He clapped

Jimmy on the back. 'Good on you, Jimmy. Dad would've been proud of you.'

Arthur's words gave Jimmy a warm glow. Yeah, maybe Dad would've been proud. It was a bonzer thought to keep inside of him.

'Come on,' Arthur said, 'let's go and clean up the backyard for Mum. It's nearly time to get the veggie garden going for summer.'

Jimmy spent the rest of the day with Arthur, and he didn't even care that he ended up doing all the heavy work and Arthur sat on the back steps and did all the bossing around. It helped to keep his mind off Bill. He didn't dare go out into the street.

When Jimmy was having a break, sitting on the steps with a cup of cold water, Arthur said, 'So you're playing a bit of footy now, are you?'

'Just with Frank and the others,' Jimmy said. He carefully didn't look at Arthur's missing leg.

'Are you any good?' Arthur asked. ''Cause if you're my brother, you'd better be. Someone's got to keep up the family name on the footy field.'

'I've kicked a few goals,' Jimmy admitted. 'But it's just a bit of fun, you know.'

'Well . . . ' Arthur paused, watching a chook scratch in the dirt. 'Maybe I might come and give you lads a bit of coaching one day. What d'you reckon?'

'That'd be beaut!' Jimmy said. 'And, er . . . ' He pointed at the chooks. 'Do you reckon we should get some more chooks? Good money in eggs. You'd have to look after them, though.'

'I think I could just about manage that,' Arthur said, and gave Jimmy a friendly punch on the arm.

By the time Mum came home, the garden was dug over and the hens had a new roof on their house.

'Did you hear the news?' Mum said as she took off her hat and re-pinned her hair.

Jimmy's stomach twisted and he and Arthur

glanced at each other. 'No, Mum. What?'

'Bill Prosser and his gang tried to rob the payroll down at the fertiliser works this morning.' She shook her head. 'What a great to-do it was. Police everywhere, and someone even said there were guns!'

Jimmy's knuckles were white on the spade he was cleaning. So it was a robbery. What a narrow squeak he'd had! 'How did the police catch them?'

'I met Sergeant Ross on my way home,' she said, and blushed. 'He's asked me to tea on Saturday afternoon.'

'What did he say about the robbery?' Arthur asked.

'Oh. Well . . . ' Mum shrugged. 'He said he'd been watching Bill for a few days, and there'd been some odd things going on – known criminals going to and fro from his house, so he suspected something was up.' She hung up her coat. 'But he wouldn't have guessed what, except that . . . Apparently Bill's young cousin, Hector, was involved. Did you ever hear such a thing – so young!'

'Hector?' Jimmy was stunned. Had Bill called Hector in after Jimmy had refused? He didn't like Hector, but he wouldn't wish gaol on him!

'Hector was on his bicycle racing off with the bag of money, but when he saw Sergeant Ross on the corner he got such a fright he crashed into the lamp post. The money went everywhere!' Mum shook her head. 'The sergeant said Hector spilled the beans straightaway.'

'Spilled the beans,' Jimmy echoed, his mind whirling. That could've been him!

Mum swung around and gave Jimmy a stern glare. 'Sergeant Ross assured me that you had no part in it, I was glad to hear. And you won't be going near Bill Prosser or his like again, will you?'

Jimmy shook his head smartly. He wasn't about to explain to Mum how close he had come to being in the lockup along with Bill and his gang! 'I'll be out looking for a new job, though,' he said.

Mum sighed. 'I do wish you'd go back to school, son.'

Arthur cleared his throat. 'Well, he might be able to soon. It's maybe time I thought about finding a bit of work,' he said. 'I'm going to get more chooks, like Jimmy suggested. And, er . . . Mr Wimple did say the other night that if I brush up on my arithmetic and writing a bit, I might be able to get on where he works. Mrs Wimple said she'd help me.'

Mum's mouth dropped open. 'I thought you told him you wouldn't go near a job like that.'

Arthur flushed. 'Well, maybe I had to hit rock bottom before I could see my way up again, eh?'

'Seems like we should do a bit of celebrating,' Mum said. She went out to the washhouse and came back holding a dusty bottle. 'The last bottle of ginger beer!'

'Careful, Mum, you're living dangerously now,' Arthur said with a laugh.

Jimmy smiled. Living dangerously? They'd all done quite enough of that this year!

When I was a kid, all I knew was that Grandad was in the war in the desert and his brother was killed on the Western Front. It was only when I started researching for this book that I began to realise there was so much more to discover about them.

The internet is a wonderful thing when it comes to family history – or any kind of history! I found both their military records and also a photo of my great-uncle that I had never seen before. Suddenly they had stories that I could learn about and imagine.

What was it like for two lads from the farm to go off to war? How did their family feel when only one came home? And what did my grandfather experience in the field ambulance unit in Egypt, seeing so many injured soldiers coming back from Gallipoli?

I named my characters Arthur and Jimmy after my grandad and his brother, and through writing this book I feel much closer to them.

I also loved the opportunity to set Jimmy's story in Yarraville. There are so many original old buildings and houses still there, and I spent a whole day walking around taking photos and getting a feel for what it used to be like during that time.

In 1915 Yarraville was very much still a working-class suburb, with lots of factories down on the Maribyrnong River. The biggest industries were the fertiliser works and the sugar factory, and other places men worked included wheelwrights, the glass factory, rope making and the acid and bone mills. Up until 1914, Yarraville was booming, even though it was surrounded by paddocks! The people who lived here felt their suburb was special and wanted to secede from being part of Footscray. There were fifty shops, several major banks, cricket and football clubs, and a brass band.

World War I changed many things, not least because so many men enlisted and went off to fight. It meant emptier streets and shops, and a shortage of workers. News from the war was scarce, and much of it was censored so that Australians knew very little of the devastating losses at Gallipoli until several months later. The terribly injured soldiers coming home on the hospital ships were a shock to many people. It became common for people to crowd around the newspaper offices, waiting for the next edition to come out to learn what was happening.

Even football suffered during the war. In 1915, the VFL competition went ahead, but St Kilda changed their colours so as to be different from those of the German Empire. Teams lacked in players because many of them were fighting overseas. In 1916 only four teams played in the competition, and although Fitzroy finished the season in last place, they won the Grand Final!

Hundreds of wounded soldiers were transported from the shores of Egypt and Turkey and nursed for weeks or even months on hospital ships anchored off-shore.

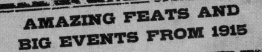

AMAZING FEATS AND BIG EVENTS FROM 1915

- On April 25, 1915, the ANZACs landed on the Gallipoli Peninsula, now known as ANZAC Cove, to battle the Turkish army.
- Charlie Chaplin's film *The Tramp* was released.
- British and German forces agreed to a Christmas Day truce in 1914, during which they played a football game in no man's land, but the following year they were forbidden to do it again.
- The United States House of Representatives rejected a proposal to give women the right to vote.
- Albert Jacka became the first Australian to win the Victoria Cross during WWI.
- The prototype military tank was first tested by the British Army.
- Einstein's theory of general relativity was formulated.